Dear Brio Girl,

Imagine this: You're driving on your favorite Interstate Highway and notice a big yellow sign that says WARNING: Steep cliff ahead. You're so ticked off, you get out of the car and scream at the top of your lungs, "How dare they put a warning sign here? Who do they think they are trying to tell me what to watch out for!?!"

Reality check: Okay, wouldn't happen. Instead of being angry, you'd actually be grateful the Department of Transportation cared enough about you to post the warning sign.

Real life: God, too, gives us warnings—not to take the fun out of life—but to protect us.

Your decision: How you respond to those warnings is up to you . . . but you need to know that your actions always determine the consequences. Good choices, good consequences. Bad choices, bad consequences. Wanna know more? Spend some time hanging with Solana. She has quite a bit to say!

Your Friend,

Susie Shellenberger, BRIO Editor
www.briomag.com

P.S. Parental review is recommended for younger readers due to themes involving premarital sex.

Brio Girls

● ● ●

Stuck in the Sky
by Lissa Halls Johnson

Fast Forward to Normal
by Jane Vogel

Opportunity Knocks Twice
by Lissa Halls Johnson

Double Exposure
by Kathy Wierenga

Good-Bye to All That
by Jeanette Hanscome

Grasping at Moonbeams
by Jane Vogel

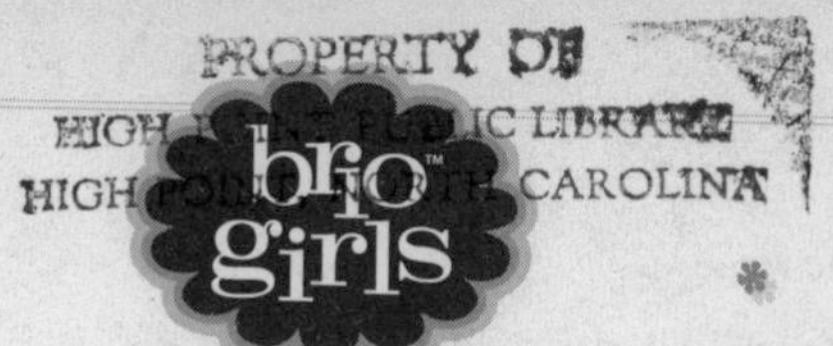

Good-Bye to All That

Created by
LISSA HALLS JOHNSON
WRITTEN BY JEANETTE HANSCOME

BETHANY HOUSE
MINNEAPOLIS, MINNESOTA

Cover design by Lookout Design Group, Inc.

Focus on the Family books are available at special quantity discounts when purchased in bulk by corporations, organizations, churches, or groups. Special imprints, messages, and excerpts can be produced to meet your needs. For more information, contact: Resource Sales Group, Focus on the Family, 8605 Explorer Drive, Colorado Springs, CO 80920; phone (800) 932-9123.

A Focus on the Family book.
Published by Bethany House Publishers
A Ministry of Bethany Fellowship International
11400 Hampshire Avenue South
Bloomington, Minnesota 55438
www.bethanyhouse.com

Printed in the United States of America by
Bethany Press International, Bloomington, Minnesota 55438

Library of Congress Cataloging-in-Publication Data

Hanscome, Jeanette.
Good-bye to all that / created by Lissa Halls Johnson ; written by Jeanette Hanscome.
p. cm. — (Brio girls)
"A Focus on the Family book."
Summary: Tired of dating jerks, Solana vows not to date until the right guy comes along but when he does, she faces the decision of whether she's ready to go all the way, amid objections from her Christian friends.
ISBN 1-58997-051-9
[1. Dating (Social customs)—Fiction. 2. Interpersonal relations—Fiction. 3. Christian life—Fiction. 4. Science—Exhibitions—Fiction. 5. High schools—Fiction. 6. Schools—Fiction.] I. Johnson, Lissa Halls, 1955- II. Title. III. Series.
PZ7.V8672 Go 2002
[Fic]—dc21 2002004563

Thanks to my family
and to all of my precious
brothers and sisters in Christ,
who supported, encouraged,
and prayed for me
as I wrote this book.
Each one of you
is a gift from God!

JEANETTE HANSCOME lives with her husband, Norm, and sons, Christian and Nathan, in Reno, Nevada. Her fiction stories, articles and devotions have appeared in Christian magazines for both teens and adults. When she isn't writing or spending time with her "boys" Jeanette enjoys serving in the music and drama ministries at First Evangelical Free Church. Whatever time is left over she spends leading a small writers critique group, taking long walks, reading whatever she can get her hands on, and hanging out with the amazing friends that God has blessed her with.

chapter 1

JOURNAL

march 12

THE BIG NIGHT

I'm so excited! I'm going out with—can you believe this?—Cameron morelli!

my friends have been giving me a hard time for making a big deal about Cameron. Becca asked what the big deal was about THIS guy. Is she blind?! Okay, so I've dated a lot of guys. I admit it. Well, this time is going to be different because Cameron is different. As proof, look what he's got planned. First, we're having dinner at a new Italian restaurant—Da Vinci's—then we're going to the Denver Observatory. So long to jerks, drive-thru burgers, and predictable action movies—this is going to be the start of something bigger and better.

Solana Luz's mind raced back, remembering her last few dates. Gregg laughed at her for being excited about her science project. Allan told her that he only dates girls with great legs—so didn't she feel privileged that he thought hers were good enough? Worst of all, Jeff wondered if "new trons" were so new, how could Solana possibly know so much about them already?

Solana sighed. "Neutrons, Jeff, are not new," she said. After half an hour of trying to explain, she gave up.

Cameron is far more intelligent than those idiots I've been dating. He gets straight A's and is in AP Chemistry with me. I bet when I say something tonight, he won't stare at me with a blank look that says, "Huh? What did that mean? Can we just make out now?"

Nope. Cameron's not just another beautiful face and hot body. He's got an attractive brain to match. It's about time.

Solana glanced at her watch and gasped. *I only have an hour until Cameron gets here.*

She sprang out of her desk chair and made a mad dash for the bathroom, taking the fastest shower possible to leave plenty of time to fix her hair and makeup.

After drying off, she threw open her closet door and removed the dress her friend Jacie had found for her while working at Raggs by Razz. She'd done a good job picking it out. As a rule, Solana thought, Jacie's tastes tended to be too conservative. But Solana had to admit—Jacie had a sharp eye for style. Even though the hem of this dress was longer than Solana usually wore—falling just above her knees—she couldn't deny that the fit and style of the dress flattered her figure perfectly. She turned to admire herself in the full-length mirror from all sides. She nodded her approval. "Jacie, you did good, *amiga*," she said aloud to the empty room.

Earlier in the afternoon, when Jacie dropped off the dress, she also dropped a few not-so-subtle hints. She followed Solana to her room. As she hung up the dress and smoothed the fabric, she spoke without looking at Solana. "Even though Cameron has more brains than most of your other dates, you still have to be careful."

"Don't worry. I'll look both ways before crossing the parking lot," Solana said.

Jacie spun around. "Don't play dumb with me," she scolded playfully. Then she hesitated, biting her lip as she always did before blurting out what she really wanted to say. "You know you *do* tend to move a little fast."

"It won't be like that with Cameron. We actually have things to talk about so we don't have to end up making out." Solana paused. "It doesn't mean we *won't* end up making out. We just won't *have* to."

Jacie shook her head, laughing. "You're hopeless."

"Yeah. And you love it."

● ● ●

By 5:55 Solana was nearly ready. She put on a second coat of Wildfire lipstick, smacked her lips, and checked her teeth for smears. She stood back from the mirror and studied herself one last time. Fluffing up her dark hair, she decided not to add more curl. "You look good, girl," she said to her reflection. "Irresistible."

Just then the doorbell rang. Grabbing a bottle of Contradiction perfume off her dresser, Solana sprayed the air twice. She spun around under the falling fragrance. *One can never smell too nice for a hot date.*

"Okay, Cameron Morelli," she whispered. "I'm ready for a good time."

● ● ●

Cameron steered his tan Blazer into the parking lot of Da Vinci's. Solana peered out her window and scanned the rows of cars, hoping to see an empty space. The smoke from Cameron's cigarette was about to choke her. She had no idea that he smoked. Had she known, she would have had second thoughts about going out with him. *Well, it's too late for that now*, she thought. *Make the best of the night. Besides, he* is *awfully cute. I'm sure it will be fine.* She admired his sandy brown hair and freshly shaved face. *Yes, cute makes up for a lot.*

She heard Cameron swear under his breath. She shot him a sideways glance. Since she wasn't immune to popping off an occasional swear word herself, some swearing didn't bother her. But she hated when people swore for no good reason. And she'd never heard Cameron talk like that.

They circled the crowded lot several times in silence. Up to this point they'd talked about school, chemistry class, and the upcoming science fair—stuff that would have put her last few dates to sleep.

She decided she needed to get Cameron talking again. She remembered an article Jacie showed her from a teen magazine titled "Ten Ways to Make a Guy Glad He's with You." One of the ways was to ask him about his car. Solana made fun of the article at the time, but *desperate times call for desperate measures*. She took a deep breath. "This is a nice Blazer." Solana ran her hand over the soft brown fabric of the front seat. "Is it yours or your dad's?"

"It's mine." Cameron grinned proudly. "I worked full-time last summer to save up for the down payment."

"Did you buy it new?"

"What kind of summer job do you think I had?" he snapped. "Junior CEO or something? It's a '96."

Solana scrunched her eyes shut for a moment, realizing how stupid she looked. Of course the Blazer wasn't new. *Then again, Cameron didn't have to be so rude about it.* "Well, it's nice anyway."

Cameron pointed at a family piling into a Taurus. "Here's our chance," he announced. "Anyone takes that space and their car's history."

Solana played along. "Calm down, tough guy," she said, patting her date on the shoulder.

Cameron turned to Solana, looking at her with purpose in his usually soft hazel eyes. He flashed a Hollywood-style grin—the grin that Solana had fallen in love with in chemistry class. "You think I'm kidding? No one's taking that spot but me."

Solana forced her lips into a tight smile, then turned her focus frontward, irritated by Cameron's bully act. At the same time, she wanted to laugh. *If only guys knew how stupid they look when acting as if they're starring in an action movie.*

The family took several minutes to get situated in their car. Suddenly, Cameron hit the horn. "What's the deal?" he hollered, as if they could hear him. "How long does it take to get two kids into seat belts?"

Solana felt her insides tighten with frustration.

Finally, the family backed their car out of the space and Cameron sped in. He got out and slammed his door. After a few seconds, Solana heard him call from behind the car, "Are you coming?"

I guess chivalry is dead, she thought. She opened her door, slid out of the truck, and caught up with her date. A heavy silence hovered between them as they walked into the restaurant.

Cameron led her through the jam-packed waiting area inside Da Vinci's to speak to the tall, elegant, dark-haired host.

"Hey." Cameron leaned on the podium. "We need a table for two please, smoking, preferably by the window." He wrapped his arm around Solana. "As you can see, I have a beautiful date to impress here."

What a pro, Solana thought sarcastically. *I hate it when guys suck up—as if it makes them look cool.* Then again, it did sound nice to hear him call her *beautiful.*

"Do you have a reservation?" the host asked.

"No," Cameron answered with bold confidence, like eating at trendy restaurants was something he did every day.

The host regarded them coolly. "Without a reservation, on weekends the wait is generally an hour. Tonight we have a 90-minute wait."

Solana dreaded Cameron's response.

"That's so lame!" Cameron snapped. He dropped his arm from around Solana and straightened up.

Solana wanted to disappear. She took a step back but kept her eyes glued to Cameron.

"What do you guys think this is anyway, some celebrity hangout in Aspen?"

"No, sir. I think we're a brand-new, very popular restaurant."

"Well, I'm a guy who wants to eat."

Solana crossed her arms, embarrassed and angry.

"Well, then." The host leaned toward Cameron. "I suggest you give me your name and find a place to wait. It will be at least 90 minutes. *At least.*"

Solana turned slowly, only to feel Cameron tug her elbow. "Come on," he said loudly. "Let's blow this place."

"Why?" Solana pulled her arm away. "It's not a big deal to wait." She glanced back at the host and offered him an apologetic smile, which he returned with a frown and roll of his eyes. *On second thought, Cameron's big mouth might get us kicked out.* "Never mind," she agreed. "Let's go."

The smell of garlic followed them out the door into the cold March air. Solana moved her short legs fast to keep up with Cameron's bold strides. Once in the truck, Cameron swore again, this time not bothering to keep it under his breath. He reached into his shirt pocket, removing a pack of cigarettes and a lighter.

"Where do you want to go?" Cameron tapped out a cigarette and lit it, tossing the pack on the seat between them. His eyes were fixed in a scowl, like a little kid who didn't get his own way.

Solana shrugged, thinking, *Home would be nice*. "Anywhere," she told him, waving away a smoke cloud that Cameron exhaled. "It doesn't matter."

After driving around for 20 minutes, they ended up at La Cocina, a cheap Mexican restaurant not far from Solana's house.

Before getting out of the truck, Cameron flicked his cigarette butt out the window. Solana's mouth fell open in disgust.

"Come on," he said before she could comment. "I'm hungry."

Once they were seated, Solana tried to hide her disappointment as she studied the plastic-covered menu. *I could have had this food at home.* She decided on beef enchiladas, knowing they wouldn't be half as good as Mama's homemade ones.

After taking their order, the waiter returned with their drinks, a basket of tortilla chips, and a dish of salsa. Cameron immediately dug in.

"So," he said, bits of chip falling from his mouth. "Here we are."

"Yeah." Solana plucked a chip out of the basket. She tried to muster up some enthusiasm and, at the same time, tune out the canned music that blasted through the sound system.

Cameron reached across the table and took Solana's other hand. "Listen, I'm sorry for acting like such a jerk earlier."

Solana wanted to say something like "Hey, you can't help the personality you were born with. I just wish I'd gotten to know the real you before I agreed to go out." But she decided to give him a break. They still had dinner and a trip to the observatory to get through.

"Don't worry about it." She dragged her chip through the dish of thin salsa. "What was the problem back there anyway?"

She felt Cameron giving her hand a squeeze. "Ah, I was just ticked off. That dude in Da Vinci's was a snob, and he treated us like dumb kids. I hate that."

Solana chuckled. "Well, you *were* kind of acting like one."

Cameron dropped Solana's hand, then held both of his up in the air, as if calling a truce. "Whoa, I'm trying to make up. Let's not fight on our first date."

"You're right," she sighed and once again forced a smile. "Let's start over."

"Great." Cameron loaded another chip with salsa and popped the whole thing into his mouth. "So, I hear you're a model."

Solana's jaw dropped. "Since when?"

"Some of the guys were saying that you sometimes get your picture in a magazine for teen girls or something like that."

"Oh," Solana finally caught on. "*Brio.* Yeah, Tyler Jennings's mom works for the magazine. Sometimes she uses him, Becca, Jacie, Hannah, and me in photo shoots. It's not like I've been in *CosmoGirl* or anything." Solana gestured like it was no big deal, while inside she thought, *Wow, some of the guys think I'm a model. Cool.*

"Well, you're hot enough to be in *CosmoGirl*."

"Thanks." Solana took a long drink of water. She studied Cameron's eyes, trying to figure out whether he was serious or just feeding her a line.

Cameron leaned back in his seat. "So, what's the deal with these friends you hang out with? I mean, they don't seem like your type."

"Why? What's wrong with them? Becca, Jacie, and Tyler have been my friends forever. Since fourth grade. Hannah's new. She's a little different, but she's okay."

"Is she that cute blonde?"

Solana nodded. "That would be Hannah."

"Man, my grandma dresses cooler than she does."

I should stand up for Hannah, Solana thought as she bit into another chip. *Sure Hannah's holier-than-thou attitude can be beyond annoying, but she does have good qualities. She stands up for what she believes in. She doesn't change herself to please other people—even if it means they think she's weird. And I must admit she's more fun to be with now than she was at first. Especially since the ski trip.*

Cameron leaned forward a little. "I heard your friends are a bunch of religious fanatics."

"Not quite. They're Christians."

"Are you into that stuff too?"

Solana shook her head hard. "No. Well, my family's Catholic. One of my uncles is even a priest. I decided a long time ago, though, that organized religion isn't for me. I mean, I believe in God. I just don't want that to be what my life is about. I believe that everyone needs to create a spirituality that works for them."

Cameron laughed before taking a few gulps of his Coke. "I bet your friends are always trying to convert you."

"Well, they do bring up God a lot. Still, they know when to lay off when they're around me."

Cameron shrugged. "Well, that's cool. I don't get that Tyler Jennings, though. What kind of guy hangs out with a bunch of girls?" With one hand he poked his straw around in his glass. "On second thought, I have a good idea what kind of guy."

Solana shot a venomous glare across the table. Where did this kid get off tearing her friends apart? He didn't even know them. "Hey, leave Tyler alone. He's a good friend. He's really been there for my friends and me. And just to get your brain back to the truth, Tyler dated Jessica Abbott for a year. I also happen to know he has a thing for Hannah."

Cameron raised one eyebrow then laughed. "He went from a girl as hot as Jessica to one as uptight as *Hannah?* Now I *know* there's something wrong with the guy."

Solana folded her arms and leaned against the back of her seat.

"Maybe we'd better keep my friends out of this. I'm pretty protective of them."

"Yeah." Cameron cleared his throat. "I can see I'm not scoring any points, and if I'm going to get what I want out of this night, I have a lot of making up to do."

Solana sat up like a shot. "*Excuse* me?"

Cameron flashed his famous smile again. This time Solana wanted to smack it right off his face. "Oh, come on. You don't have to play innocent with me. Guys talk, and you have quite a reputation."

"A reputation for what?" Solana knew it was no secret that she kissed and fooled around sometimes. But it sounded like Cameron had more on his mind than that.

He leaned in closer. "Don't act like you're still a virgin."

"Actually, I am." Solana felt heat rising in her cheeks.

"Not according to what I hear."

She fought to keep her self-control. "Why are you listening to what other people say? I thought you were an intelligent guy. Don't you have better things to do with your time than waste it on locker room trash-talk?"

Cameron laughed and combed his fingers through his hair. "I may be an intelligent guy, but I'm still a *guy*—"

"You got that right!"

"—a guy who's interested in a girl like you."

That's it! Solana snatched up her purse and jumped from her seat. Grabbing her jacket from the back of the seat, she thrust her arms into it.

"Hey!" Cameron said. "What's going on?"

"I'm leaving."

"Why? The evening just started."

Solana snorted in disgust. "Well, mine's over."

"What about the observatory?"

"Oh, like I want to stand in the dark with you, knowing what's on your mind?"

"What about dinner?"

"I lost my appetite." She dug into her purse for some money and tossed a few bills onto the table. "That should cover my order."

"You're going to walk all the way home?"

Solana nodded, her now-limp curls bobbing down her back. "We're in my neighborhood, you idiot. It's only a few blocks. I'll survive." With that, Solana stomped out of the restaurant.

Outside she stopped in her tracks. Papa would have a fit if she walked home alone in the dark. Besides that, she hated to walk. She considered calling her parents. No, then she'd have to risk Cameron's coming outside for another soap opera moment while she waited for them. Solana fastened the snaps on her jacket, wishing she'd worn something warmer. This jacket was more for looks than warmth and, combined with her short skirt, was not much protection from the cold. *At least it's not snowing.*

Shoving her hands into her shallow pockets, Solana started walking. Light snowflakes began to swirl down from the sky.

She blinked against them. *Perfect.*

chapter 2

On Monday morning Solana kept her gaze straight ahead as she made her way to the Stony Brook High School cafeteria, moving in an even bolder version of her trademark strut. So far she'd managed to avoid Cameron Morelli. The cafeteria might be another story. And she still had to figure out how to deal with him during seventh period chemistry.

Cameron's face flashed through Solana's mind. She gave her raspberry gum a couple of tension-releasing chomps, then a loud snap. *I can't believe I used to think his face was so gorgeous. Now if I saw it, I'd throw up.*

"Solana, over here!"

Her pace slowed at the sound of Becca's voice. She spotted Becca across the food-court-style lunchroom, waving her arm with such enthusiasm that her brown ponytail swung from side to side. Solana navigated through the maze of tables to join her friend who'd claimed a spot in the far corner with Hannah, Jacie, and Tyler. She tossed her backpack onto the bench before taking the empty place beside Jacie.

"I'm *so* glad to see you guys." Solana glanced around the table. "Where were you yesterday? I called each of you and no one was home." She unzipped her backpack to retrieve her lunch.

"Church," they all said.

"Family," Hannah added.

"I *needed* you," Solana complained.

"So, how was the big date?" Jacie asked.

Solana set her paper lunch bag in front of her, ripped off a piece, and wrapped her gum in it. "Don't ask!"

Becca laid down her half-eaten sandwich. "That good, huh? What happened to, 'Cameron's different from all the other guys I've dated'? I think *special* was the word you used."

"He's special all right. A special type of mutant pond scum." Solana acted like she was gagging. "Take my advice, *mis amigas*—if Cameron ever flashes that smile in your direction, run for your life."

Becca and Tyler smirked through mouths full of food.

"I'll remember that," Hannah said, unwrapping some orange slices.

Jacie gave Solana a compassionate pat on the arm. "I'm sorry," she said.

"Yeah, thanks."

"So?" Becca said, leaning across the table. "Spill it."

"It's not a pretty story," Solana said.

Tyler shrugged. "I like 'em better when they're not pretty."

"Then you go out with him," she said. "You can have your own ugly story to tell."

"That bad?" Becca asked.

"Let me put it this way—some species of bacteria have better manners than he does." She went on to recount the entire story of Cameron's rude behavior in Da Vinci's and the parking lot. She told them about ending up at the cheap Mexican restaurant. When she got to the part where Cameron asked about her modeling career, the whole table erupted. Tyler laughed so hard he almost choked on a mouthful of Dr Pepper.

"That's one of the oldest pickup lines in the book," he said, once he'd recovered. "He could have at least thought up something original."

Jacie's face spread into a huge smile, revealing her deep dimples. "Tyler, please thank your mom for making us famous."

"Hey." Tyler plunked his drink down. "When's my modeling career going to start impressing the girls?"

"I don't think any of you are famous," Solana corrected with a sly smile. "Just me." She went on to share other choice things Cameron had said, skipping the insults about her friends. Then she told them about his intentions for the evening.

"He said *what?*" Hannah wrinkled her face in disgust. She shivered the top half of her body, as if a violent chill traveled up her spine.

Becca shook her head. "What a slime bag."

"What did you do?" Jacie asked.

"Got up and left." Solana felt her anger return. "I'm so mad at myself now because I actually paid my share of the bill."

"Are you serious?" Tyler's eyes flashed in anger. "You should have made him pay."

"I didn't want him to have a reason to say I owe him anything."

"True," Jacie agreed. She tossed her long black curls behind her shoulders. For a change, she was wearing her hair down and free of any fancy braids or clips. "But I would've pretended those comments didn't bother me one bit. Then I would've made a trip to the ladies room, with a detour out the front door, straight to a phone booth where I'd have called Damien to come pick me up on his Harley."

Becca reached across the table to high-five Jacie.

"By the way, how *did* you get home, Solana?" Becca asked.

"I walked." Solana rested her arms on the table in front of her.

"Was that safe?" Hannah's eyes widened with concern.

Solana rolled her eyes. "Hannah, you are such a mother."

Jacie spoke up. "Hannah's right. Some psycho could've picked you up."

"That wouldn't have been any worse than sitting in a booth with one." Solana took a sip of her drink. "Besides, I got home in one piece. So relax. And you can save the lecture. Papa gave me one at home. He told me that if this kind of thing ever happens again, I'd better call him so he can pick me up *and* have some words with my date. Well, he doesn't have to worry about that because there aren't going to be any more dates for a long time."

A hush fell over the table. They all looked at Solana, as if waiting for the punch line. Tyler finally said, "Yeah, right, Solana."

Becca picked up her sandwich. "She's just kidding."

Solana sat up very straight. "I am not!" She pulled a foil-wrapped quesadilla out of her bag and opened it. "I've had my fill of jerks. All the guys at this school are losers." Tyler cleared his throat and she added, "Except you, Tyler."

"Thanks, Sol," he said, giving her an exaggerated grin.

"And Nate," Becca added. "He's definitely another exception."

"Fine, Nate's okay too. And in case you were about to throw a fit, Jacie, I'll include Damien on the list of non-jerks. But as far as the rest of them go . . ." Solana made a thumbs-down gesture with both hands.

"Sure," Becca said, picking up her sandwich again. "Until the next good-looking senior walks by."

"No, my mind is made up," Solana insisted. She took a large bite of her quesadilla.

"Uh-huh, Solana, sure." Jacie nodded. "We believe you."

With her mouth full, Solana mumbled, "No you don't."

"You're right; we don't!" Jacie quickly bit into a carrot stick.

Hannah looked at Solana, her eyes twinkling with mischief. "Well, since you're giving up dating, maybe you'll decide to opt for courtship after all."

"Or maybe *not*."

"Name one thing that's so horrible about it," Hannah challenged, teasing in her voice.

"The word courtship to begin with," Solana said with an exaggerated Southern accent. "I picture myself on a porch swing, sipping lemonade with some hick named Billy Ray Jim Bob."

Becca leaned in. "Can you see your dad, watching from the window with a shotgun in case the boy gets fresh and tries to hold your hand?"

Solana dropped her jaw and opened her eyes extra wide. "No, not hand-holding! Oh, Becca, get your mind out of the gutter!" she gasped dramatically.

Another chorus of laughter rose from the group. Even Hannah choked back a giggle. "It's not that bad."

Jacie nudged Solana in the ribs with her elbow. "Aw, you don't need Billy Ray Jim Bob to court you when you've got Dennis Sanchez, your secret love."

"Yeah," Solana rolled her eyes. "That ranks right up there with my 'secret love' for gerbil barf."

"I love watching him give you those puppy dog looks." Jacie grabbed both of Solana's hands, pulled them close to her and batted her big brown eyes. She lowered her voice to imitate Dennis. "Oh, Solana, my darling lab partner, please notice the love in my eyes and say you feel it too."

Solana yanked her hands away, clutching them to her chest. "Oh, Dennis! I *do* have love for you in my eyes." She batted her eyes. "Wait a second." She touched a finger to the edge of her eye, then inspected it. "No . . . that's just a piece of fuzz. Sorry."

Solana shook her head. "I just wish he could get it through his thick head that I only think of him as a friend. All we have in common is a fascination with science."

"That's perfect," Tyler said. "Because he's got Dennis and Solana 'chemistry' on the brain."

"Well," Solana said with conviction, "if he wants to go out with me, he's got a long wait. Dating is no longer a part of my life."

"Just like me," Hannah said. "There's only one man out there I need to fall in love with."

"Whoa, there!" Solana said, putting up her hands. "It's not like I'm waiting to date until Mr. Future Husband walks in. The way I see it, I'm not going to go out with just anyone again. I'm going to hold out for the right guy—someone who goes beyond looks and brains. One who's worth spending time with." Solana tucked her long hair behind her ears. *It would also be nice to have a guy who actually cares more about me than his hormones.*

Becca looked amused. "What happened to a guy just being a great kisser?"

"Yeah, well, that was nice, but look where it got me," Solana protested. "I'm being trash-talked in the locker room." She looked down at her half-eaten lunch, then up at Tyler. "Do all the guys think of me as easy?"

Tyler looked away.

"Solana, you should have set Cameron straight," Hannah said forcefully. "You should have told him that even though you kiss, you won't have sex until your wedding night. Maybe that would have gotten around the locker room."

Tyler shook his head almost imperceptibly.

"Well, I don't necessarily believe that," Solana said. "I probably *will* have sex before I'm married."

Nobody said anything. They just looked at each other.

"Come on," Solana said. "Don't act so shocked. You guys are probably the only ones who won't have sex before you're married.

This is the way things are now. It's accepted. There's nothing wrong with sex."

"Well, at least you're right about *that*," Jacie said.

Now everyone stared at Jacie.

"Well, there's not," Jacie said. "Sex isn't wrong. It's when and who with that's the wrong part. It's only the context that's wrong."

"And what is the wrong context?" Solana challenged.

"Anything that's not inside marriage," Jacie retorted. "Sex is for a husband and wife only. You need to wait, Sol."

Solana snorted. She stared into Jacie's eyes. "I'm sorry, but I think you have me confused with one of your fellow Puritans. Remember, this is the twenty-first century."

"Some truths don't change over time," Tyler said.

Throwing her hands up, Solana asked, "What's the big deal? I'm not telling you guys to do it."

"Solana, the Bible is full of reasons why it's a big deal," Hannah informed her. "The book of Hebrews says that the marriage bed is to be kept sacred."

"*Sacred?*" Solana sneered. "It sounds like a couple has to sprinkle their bed with holy water or something."

"Jacie's right," Becca said. "God made sex for husbands and wives as a beautiful expression of their love for each other."

Solana rolled her eyes.

"Come on, Solana. Be serious."

"Okay, Becca, I see your point on part of it. It's totally important that two people be in love and committed before they have sex. Even I don't understand how girls can do it with guys they don't care about. Why do you think I was so mad that Cameron thought I'd done it already? Well, you can be sure that when I do have sex for the first time, it won't be with someone like him."

Solana looked at her friends, their concerned looks aggravating, rather than pleasing her. "But saying the couple has to be married is, like, something out of the Dark Ages. Or the fifties! Almost nobody thinks that way anymore."

Becca raised an eyebrow. "More people believe in saving sex for marriage than you think."

Tyler pushed the hair out of his eyes and looked intensely at Solana. "The world makes sex seem like no big deal, like it's just another type of affection or something. But there's more to it than that."

"And you know this from your own personal experience? Do you have something to confess?"

Tyler turned red. "I'm part of the locker room crowd, remember? I know what goes on in there. I know the attitudes these guys have."

Solana wouldn't let herself admit that he could be right. Then they'd think she agreed with everything. She sat stone-faced.

"You aren't going to listen to anything we say, are you?" Tyler looked frustrated.

"Well," Solana said, reaching for her backpack. "You forget: I don't let the Bible dictate my life. Do I expect you to live according to the rules of Hispanic culture? No. It's great that you think of sex as sacred and all that, but I personally believe it's up to each individual person. I do think sex is special. And that's why I plan to wait for the right person, someone I'm really in love with, someone who feels the same about me."

Becca clasped her hands in front of her on the table. "If you don't care what the Bible has to say, then what about the other real-life stuff—like getting pregnant?"

"Don't insult my intelligence, Becca. I wouldn't be stupid enough to do anything without protection."

"Getting pregnant doesn't always mean the two people are stupid," Jacie said. "Or that they didn't use protection."

My big mouth gets me in trouble again. Solana saw the hurt on Jacie's face. Jacie was so sensitive about the fact that her parents had never married. "Sorry, Jace." Solana faced her. "You're right . . ."

"Besides, protection doesn't always work, Solana," Becca said, her voice hard.

Solana took a breath, but Hannah spoke up with a question that shocked everyone. "What if the guy has a disease, like chlamydia or AIDS?" Hannah asked.

Everyone turned to stare at her.

"I just got out of that stupid health class, remember?"

"I'll know him well enough to be absolutely sure he doesn't have anything like that."

"What if he decides not to tell you?" Tyler asked. "Or lies about it?"

"He won't." Solana looked into the faces of her worried friends. With all their strong convictions, how could she ever make them understand? *I'd better shut up. I shouldn't have brought it up in the first place*. "Don't worry about me doing anything today. Like I said before, I'm taking a break from the dating scene anyway." She paused. "Look, you guys, just be happy I'm making this one good decision not to date every guy who comes along, okay? It'll be a long time before anything else happens."

"How do you plan on filling up your extra time?" Hannah gathered the lunch trash from the table.

"For one, I plan to spend a little more time hanging out with my friends." Solana stuffed her trash into her paper bag.

"Does that mean I can count on you to be at my basketball game this Friday?" Becca looked hopeful as she slung her backpack over one shoulder.

Solana pretended she was put out by the idea. She sighed and said, "Okay, I'll be at the big basketball game on Friday. I *guess* if my best friend is playing *and* the team is winning, I can work it into my calendar."

Becca pumped the air. "Yes! You've hardly been to any of my games this season."

"Don't take it personally, Bec," Tyler said. "She's been blowing off my games, too."

"I've been busy with my science fair project. Which is another thing that I plan to devote more time to. In fact, Dennis and I are getting together at his house this afternoon to work on it."

Becca and Jacie looked into each other's eyes. "Ooo!" they said at the same time. Becca started making kissing sounds.

Solana wadded up a napkin and tossed it at Becca. "Will you two grow up? Dennis is a good scientist who happens to own a greenhouse and a computer program that I don't have and can't afford."

Becca threw the napkin back at Solana. "So how's it going? You haven't even told us, you've been so busy stalking Cameron the last few weeks."

"All I know," Tyler said, "is that it's about plants and acid participation."

"Acid *precipitation* on our local soil and plant life." Solana noticed that while everyone looked interested, Hannah was the only one who didn't look stumped. "I've taken it a step further and examined the acid level in the snow around here. I'm using a couple of common plants and a Colorado blue spruce sapling, along with some pasture grass, like the grass that the horses graze on at my uncle's ranch." She'd had her uncle's horses and her *puros tesoros*—the wild mustangs she followed—in mind when deciding to add pasture grass to the project.

Tyler hopped up at the sound of the bell ending lunch. "Sounds like a lot of work."

"And interesting," Hannah added. "Acid rain can be devastating. It has completely destroyed some forests in Europe, and in Vermont, too."

Solana nodded. "There's so much information to keep track of.

Plus examining the plant life and soil constantly. But it's been really interesting."

Jacie led the way to the trash cans on their way out of the lunchroom. "It's a good idea. People are always interested in projects that deal with problems affecting the area where they live."

"I hope so." Solana stuffed her trash into the full can. "If I make it to the highest level, I could even win a scholarship."

"That would be exciting!" Hannah walked beside Solana. "I'll pray for your project every day."

"We all will," Becca said.

"Thanks. I'll need it," Solana said before catching herself with her guard down. She straightened her shoulders and gave her head a toss. "Don't think admitting I need your prayers for my project means I'll ask for them all the time."

Jacie smiled at Solana. "We'd pray for you whether you wanted it or not. Anyway, someday, when you're a famous scientist, we'll all be able say, 'Hey, I know her. She's one of my best friends.' "

"Yeah," Solana said. "I'll remember that you were, uh . . . what was your name again? Janie? Janice?"

"You'd better be nice, Sol," Becca said. "Jacie's going to be a famous artist someday."

"Good point, Bertha," Solana said.

"We'll see you later," Tyler said. "Hazel and I need to get to class."

"Yeah," Hannah added. "Come on, Tyrone."

Solana watched the crowd nudge and joke their way down the hall. *Maybe dropping the dating scene will be more fun than I thought.*

chapter 3

Solana groaned and reached over to slap the beeping alarm into silence. She pulled the covers over her face. She hated having to wake up so early on a Saturday.

Why did I promise Uncle Manuel that I'd help him this *weekend?* Solana flopped her arms over the top of the covers and stared at the ceiling. Usually, she loved helping out at her uncle's horse ranch. But with the science fair only days away, all she could think of was the amount of work she still had to do.

The week since her disaster date with Cameron had flown by. To Solana's relief, Cameron only gave her occasional dirty looks in chemistry class. She felt free to ignore him and focus her energy on studying in the library, working in the Sanchez greenhouse, or using Dennis's elaborate computer system. Her only break had been the night before with the basketball game, then pizza and air hockey at Becca's afterward.

Before dragging herself out of bed, Solana studied the mural of wild mustangs that she and Jacie had painted on the wall across from her bed the previous summer.

"*Buenos días*, Alessandro," Solana whispered to the unicorn foal that ran ahead of the mustangs in the painting. "Are you taking good care of my *puros tesoros?*" She imagined the sound of thundering horses' hooves. How long had it been since she'd seen the wild mustangs that she called her "pure treasures" and tracked through the mountains?

She looked into the eyes of the unicorn foal, which she'd secretly named after her brother who died of heart disease. Since she was only two years old when Alessandro died, Solana didn't remember him. She wished she could. Many times, she'd thought about telling Mama she named the unicorn after Alessandro, that she pictured him as a kind of horse angel, looking after her treasured wild horses. Mama would like that. Still, Solana had never told Mama or anyone else.

After another yawn, Solana sat up slowly, stretched, and forced her body out of bed.

Showering woke Solana up a little, but some of the heavy grogginess refused to let go, even after she threw on jeans and a sweatshirt. While she brushed her hair into a ponytail and applied some makeup, she reviewed the day's schedule in her head.

Help Uncle Manuel until after lunch.

Go to Dennis's to check on my plants and update the charts on his computer.

Go buy the materials for my project display.

Good thing I swore off guys, she thought as she replaced the lid on her mascara. *I wouldn't have time for them anyway!*

Grabbing a denim jacket off the back of her desk chair, Solana hurried downstairs to the kitchen. The rich aroma of coffee chased the fog out of her head.

"Morning, Mama," she said, finding her mother preparing eggs.

Narina Luz gave her daughter a warm smile and a kiss on the cheek. "Good morning, *mi'ja*. You're up early."

Solana opened the cupboard over the coffeemaker and took out her favorite extra-large mug. "I promised Uncle Manuel I'd be at his place by eight. I thought about calling him and saying I'd help him after I turn in my project, but I figured that since he was nice enough to let Becca's family use the ranch for Alvaro's birthday next weekend, the least I could do is help get it ready."

"Being with the horses will be good for you—they'll get your mind off the project for a while." Mrs. Luz sprinkled some grated cheese over her pan of eggs. "Today you won't be alone. Manuel hired a new ranch hand."

Solana rolled her eyes, remembering the last couple of guys that her uncle had hired and quickly fired.

"Great," Solana muttered. *Just what I want to do—help some dumb new guy find his way around.*

"Oh, now." Narina gave her daughter's ponytail a gentle tug. "Be nice."

"I'm always nice."

"Except when you've got an attitude."

Solana poured coffee into her mug and scooped in a heaping spoonful of sugar. "Me? An attitude? Never!" She plopped onto one of the wooden chairs at the kitchen table. Her mother set a plate of eggs mixed with cheese, salsa, and a homemade tortilla in front of her.

"I like working with the horses by myself. I don't like anyone getting in my way."

"It won't be so bad," Solana's mother said. "Manuel says Ramón is a hard worker. I'm sure he'll have plenty of his own work to do and won't have time to get in your way."

"I hope so."

Solana ate quickly. Once she finished, she rinsed her dishes and stacked them in the sink. "Bye, Mama," she called after rinsing her plate. "I have to run a couple of errands when I'm done, so I'll see you later."

"How are you getting there?"

"My bike."

Solana's mother took her purse from the counter and dug around inside. "Use the car. It's cold today." She tossed the keys to Solana.

"Thanks."

"You're welcome." She waved a hand to dismiss her daughter. "Now go before you're late."

● ● ●

In the cold, crisp morning air, the smell of horses and fresh hay was like heaven. When Solana caught sight of the pen full of horses, she felt ready to get her mind off the science project for a few hours.

"*Hola*, *Tio* Manuel," Solana shouted, waving to her uncle in the distance. He lifted his chin in greeting since his hands were busy fastening Carmen's halter around her chin.

"Ready for some help?" She approached Carmen slowly, patting her neck underneath the wiry black and brown mane.

"Yep. I'll use all I can get."

"Thanks again for letting Becca have Alvaro's party here," Solana said. "It means a lot to her family."

"Glad to do it." Manuel rewarded Carmen's patience with a carrot stick. "The little boy deserves it after all he's been through. Losing his mother in a fire. Having all those burn treatments." Manuel shook his head.

"Well, he has a new obsession now," Solana said. "You should see him, galloping around the McKinnon house on an invisible pony, whinnying and calling 'whoa!' It's so funny."

Manuel smiled. "Now he'll be able to ride a real horse instead of the air."

"Prepare to be mobbed by seven-year-olds," Solana warned him.

"You know your Aunt Maricella. She loves kids and parties."

A tall, dark-haired boy, who looked about her age, appeared in the doorway of the stable. "The hinge on that stall door is fixed," he said, running his fingers through his short, curly hair. Solana saw him stare at her for a moment and smile shyly. "So, Manuel," he said, "did you hire an extra hand, or am I being replaced already?"

"Sorry. Ramón, this is my niece, Solana." Manuel gave Solana a quick squeeze. "Solana, this is my new hired hand, Ramón. Solana's here to give us a hand and mooch a ride on Shadow."

"Nice to meet you, Solana," Ramón said, smiling crookedly. He walked over to Solana and held out his hand. She shook it, feeling weird shaking hands with someone her own age.

"Yeah, nice to meet you, too." Solana let go of his firm grip and stuck her hand into the pocket of her jeans. *If I was paying attention to guys, I'd think you're cute.* She turned to her uncle. "So, what do you want done first?"

Manuel removed his faded baseball cap and smacked some dirt off it. "You can help Ramón clean out the stable. Then why don't you groom Shadow? When your aunt returns from church, we can get the yard and back porch looking good for next weekend."

"Okay," Solana said and started walking toward the stable.

"All right, Carmen," Manuel said to the horse, "are you ready for your makeover?"

Ramón chuckled, and Solana started laughing too.

"Your uncle is funny," Ramón said quietly. "I think Carmen's his favorite."

"He talks to all of them like that." Solana walked ahead of Ramón into the stable. *Now let's see how much this guy knows about horses.*

"Your uncle told me he named her after the opera, *Carmen*."

"That he did." Solana grabbed a pitchfork from the corner of the stable and walked toward a row of stalls in the back.

"All the horses' names have special meanings," Ramón said. "That's really cool."

"Uh-huh." *I hope he doesn't talk my ear off all morning.*

"Manuel told me that *Carmen* is the opera he took your aunt to see while they were dating and he really wanted to impress her. I'll have to keep that in mind for my next girlfriend."

Solana tried hard not to smile. She always loved hearing Manuel and Maricella share stories about their dating days.

"I know I'm too young to like opera, but Andrea Bocelli changed all that."

Solana raised her eyebrows. *Andrea Bocelli? I'm impressed.*

"Let's see." Ramón looked up. "Shadow got his name because as a foal he followed Manuel around the pen like a little shadow."

Solana didn't mean to, but she sighed loudly. She heaved a fork full of soiled straw from the floor onto a pile to throw away later. *I named Shadow. Does he think* I'm *the new one around here?*

"Sorry. I guess you know all this stuff." Ramón took off his hat and scratched the top of his head.

"Uh, yeah. I practically live here on weekends and holidays."

"Really? Then I guess we'll be hanging out together a lot."

With fake enthusiasm Solana said, "I guess."

Ramón reached for a bale of fresh hay. "Well, maybe you can help me figure out something that Manuel *didn't* fill me in on."

"Like what?"

"Why did he name this place *El Rancho de la Libèlula*? The Dragonfly Ranch seems like a strange name for a horse ranch."

Solana brushed straw off her jeans, then stood up straight. "There's a pond on the property that attracts a lot of dragonflies in the summer." She smiled to herself, picturing the place she liked to ride to on summer days to sit and think. "We call it the dragonfly pond because there are *hundreds* of them. Manuel named the ranch after that pond."

Ramón nodded. "I'll have to see it sometime."

They worked in silence for about two minutes before Ramón asked, "Are you a junior or a senior?"

"Junior," she answered without looking up from her work. "What about you?" she asked, just to be polite.

"I'm doing my first year at the UC extension here in Copper Ridge."

Well, well, a college man. I bet he hasn't even declared a major yet. If he has, it's probably something lame like PE. How smart can he be if he's scooping horse manure for a living?

"Hmm." Solana scooped another bunch of hay into her throw-away pile as Manuel went back outside.

Solana lost herself in her own thoughts while she continued to work. Ramón talked, but she didn't really pay attention to what he said, only popped in an occasional "Mmhmm" or "Yeah, really?"

When the floor of the stall was clean, Solana looked around for a wheelbarrow to load her dirty straw into. "Be right back," she said, glad to find an excuse to ditch Ramón for a few minutes. Outside, her uncle grinned like the Cheshire cat.

"Hey, Manuel, where's the wheelbarrow?"

"In the shed." He set down his grooming brush. "I'll go with you. I'm sure it's locked."

Once out of earshot of the stable, Manuel looked at Solana. "So, what do you think?" he asked.

"Think?" Solana glanced at her uncle. "Of what?"

"Of Ramón? He's nice, huh?"

Solana shrugged. "Sure, he's pretty nice. He likes to talk *a lot.*"

"Because he's interested in everything. Smart kid, like you." Manuel whistled a tune on their way to the shed. As he unlocked it, he said, "After the work is done, why don't you and Ramón take a ride? You can show him the trails."

The thought of a long ride on Shadow made Solana wish her

science project could wait. But if she went riding, she'd want to go alone anyway—not play tour guide.

"Can't," Solana told her uncle. "I have a lot of work to do on my science project. It's due Wednesday."

"That's right—the big science fair." Manuel opened the shed and pointed at the wheelbarrow. "You're a good girl to put schoolwork first. My girls put everything *but* school first. I always had to be on them about that. So you finish your project. When it's done, *then* you can give Ramón a tour of the trails, huh?"

"Yeah, yeah." Solana nodded as she pulled the wheelbarrow out of the shed. "Okay."

Manuel resumed his whistling and returned to his grooming while Solana trundled the wheelbarrow to the stable. And then the thought hit: *Is my uncle trying to set me up with Ramón? If he is, he can just forget it. I've given up guys.*

chapter 4

Solana sat on her bedroom floor looking over the final touches on her project. She had only an hour before Jacie came to help her transport it to school—and Solana hadn't even showered yet.

The night before, at Dennis's house, Solana gathered all the pieces of the project. She attached photographs of the plants, pasture grass, and blue spruce saplings taken at various stages during the study onto the backdrop. She labeled both her control group and the plants irrigated with water high in sulfuric and nitric acid. Also, Dennis helped her transplant the specimens into brand new pots—green for the control group and brown for those with a high acid level.

After she got home from Dennis's house, she thought of ways to make her backdrop more eye-catching, but it was after ten o'clock, and Mama insisted that she wait until morning.

So, before anyone else in the house was awake, Solana began cutting and gluing strips of construction paper around each photograph. While the glue dried, she added other finishing touches.

She propped up the backdrop behind two rows of pots. A label marking the green pots read: CONTROL GROUP, WATERED WITH STANDARD TAP WATER. By the brown pots the label read: WATERED WITH pH 4.0.

She stood back and studied how the project would look at school. "It looks perfect, Ms. Solana Luz," she told herself.

The written report lay on her desk in a forest green folder. Reaching for it, Solana forced her hand back. *No, don't look it over again.*

Taking a long breath, Solana smiled to herself. *Now I'm done. I hope all those months of work and research are about to pay off.*

● ● ●

"Solana, over here." Solana heard Tyler shout from somewhere in the crowded gym. Unable to see him, she stretched herself up on her tiptoes and searched through a sea of bodies until she found her friend, standing with Becca near the team bench.

Shoving her way through, she finally reached Tyler and Becca. Solana greeted them with a tired, "Hey."

Tyler cocked his head to one side. "Man, you look wiped."

"I was up at five doing last-minute work on my project," Solana said. "And I've been up 'til midnight almost every night this week finishing up the written report."

"Aw, you poor thing." Tyler stood behind Solana and massaged her shoulders. "You're going to be growing leaves pretty soon."

Becca clasped her hands and reached high over her head, stretching her muscles for the game. "Yeah . . . in fact, your hair looks a little greener today."

"Ha-ha." Solana gave Becca a phony smile. "Are you switching from sports to stand-up comedy?"

"Well, if we don't win this game, I might need to." Becca gave

Solana a playful slap on the arm. "You'd think you'd feel better now that your project is turned in."

"Yeah, well, I have two torturous days of waiting for the judging."

Tyler pressed the heel of one hand into an extra tense spot on Solana's back. "Look at it this way . . . now you have even more time to hang out with us."

Solana moved her neck and shoulders as Tyler finished his massage. "Thanks, Ty." She let out a long sigh. Having a guy in their group did have its benefits.

"Now remember," Tyler said, pointing at Becca. "Since the guys' team lost last night's game, it's up to the girls now. Make us proud."

Becca saluted Tyler. "Yes, sir!" She rolled her eyes at Solana.

Solana punched Tyler's arm. "Way to get her relaxed before the game."

"What are friends for?"

Katie Spencer trotted over to them. "Ready to win, Becca?" she asked, hopping from one foot to the other.

"Ready as always."

"Good." Katie lowered her voice. "I've heard you pray before every game."

Becca nodded. "Yep."

Katie began massaging her left shoulder with her right hand, as if trying to work out a knot. "I generally keep my spiritual walk private. But I wondered about the possibility of team prayer before each game. I'm doing a quiet poll of the girls to be sure no one feels pressured."

"That's a great idea." Becca smiled. "You can put in a 'yes' vote for me."

"And you don't mind group prayers from different kinds of girls?"

Why wouldn't it be okay? Solana narrowed her eyes in confusion as she looked from Katie to Becca. *Prayer is prayer. It all goes to the same place, right?*

"I guess not," Becca said, looking confused as well.

"Hey, Katie," Solana said, an idea suddenly coming to her. "Pray my science fair project wins too."

"Sure, no problem." Katie smiled back.

The coach waved Becca and Katie over. "Time to show Lakeview how to play basketball," Becca said, giving Katie a high-five. Together they ran to join their team.

The band began tuning up behind Solana. She turned to Tyler. "That's our cue to find a seat before the band blasts out our eardrums."

"We need to save a seat for Jacie, too. She had to work, so she'll be late."

"Where's Hannah?"

Tyler pointed to the other side of the gym. "Taking pictures for the school paper."

Together they made their way up the bleachers, finding enough space in the third section. As they sat down, Solana turned to Tyler, giving him a teasing smile. "So, you think God's gonna help us win?"

Tyler shrugged. "I think God cares more about our attitudes than about our winning."

The band broke into a rousing tune as a group of basketball cheerleaders cartwheeled onto the court.

Solana groaned at the sound of their cheers and shrieks. "Here comes the rah-rah squad. I'm so glad. My perky meter was running low."

The cheerleaders hollered, "1 . . . 2 . . . 3 . . . 4 . . . Let's go, let's score!"

Solana dabbed at her eyes. "They're counting now! I'm so proud!"

"What's wrong with the cheerleaders?" Tyler leaned forward with his eyes fixed on the energetic group of girls. "They're fun to watch."

"Oh, I wonder why. Could it be the short skirts and disgustingly perfect bodies?"

"No." Tyler shook his head. "Not at all. It's the deep, meaningful lyrics to the cheers that move me."

"Mmmmm," Solana said, smiling blissfully. "Yes, I guess that is true. It just makes you feel like your IQ soars off the charts."

She sat back and let her mind wander. Sometime later, a cheer jolted Solana out of her daze. She clapped along with the crowd, clueless about what had just happened.

Tyler yelled, "Good shot, Becca!" He turned to Solana. "That was amazing! Too bad Jacie's not here. She missed a great play."

And so did I, Solana thought ruefully. To cover, she cupped her hands around her mouth and called, "Go, Becca!"

She reached into her pocket for a piece of gum, hoping that chewing would keep her more alert. While peeling off the wrapper, she felt someone slip in beside her. She turned to tell whoever it was that the place was taken. She almost dropped her gum when she recognized him. *Tristan Fletcher.* She'd been flirting with him in English class all semester, hoping he'd ask her out.

"Hi, Solana," Tristan said.

"Hi," Solana said casually. Her instinct was to move a little closer to him and start to flirt. But she forced herself to stay put. She felt Tyler watching her. "I'm saving that spot for Jacie," Solana said before he could say anything.

"I only came over for a minute. I just wanted to know if you wanted to do something this weekend."

Great. He never asked me out when I wanted him to. No, he waits until I've sworn off guys. She took a deep breath and commanded herself: *Stick to the commitment.*

But I've waited so long . . . he's so cute . . . and he's not anything like Cameron . . . maybe just once?

chapter 5

Solana clenched her hands together. She felt Tyler's eyes boring into her. *He's waiting for me to cave in.* She looked at Tristan and smiled. "Actually, I'm really busy."

"Well, what about next weekend? I thought maybe we could go to a movie or something."

"Sorry, I can't." She looked away from his eyes and perfect, kissable lips. "I have a lot going on right now." Solana almost didn't recognize the sound of her own voice. The only times she *ever* turned a guy down was when she already had a date or didn't like him—and that was rare.

Tristan lowered his eyes and picked at a tear in his jeans. "Well, maybe sometime, when you're not so busy."

Solana smiled. "Yeah. I'll call you."

Tristan stayed beside Solana and watched the game for a few minutes before saying, "Well, I guess I'll see you later then."

"See you."

After Tristan left, Tyler let out a slow whistle. "I can *not* believe it," he said, turning toward Solana.

"I know you were waiting for me to cave in. Well, as you can see, I do have some control over my raging hormones."

Tyler draped an arm over Solana's shoulder. "I'm proud of you, Sol. If I hadn't been here to witness this historic event for myself, I never would have believed it. Wait 'til I tell Becca."

"No, please, let me spare you the trouble." Solana cupped her hands around her mouth, stood up, and shouted, "Hey, Becca, guess what . . ."

Tyler grabbed her by the back of the shirt and yanked her down. "Are you insane?"

"Maybe I am! I just turned down Tristan Fletcher."

Solana pretended to watch the game, cheering when everyone else did. Halfway into the second quarter she spotted Jacie. She stood, waved, and shouted, "We're up here, Jace!"

Jacie stepped up the bleachers, saying "hi" to several people on the way. Solana watched her and wondered how Jacie managed to be friends with practically everyone in school.

When Jacie finally sat down, Tyler leaned toward her. "Jacie, you missed it."

"Missed what?" Jacie leaned across Solana to get closer to Tyler. "Did Becca score?"

"Well, yeah. That, too. But you missed Solana's big moment. She turned down a date with Tristan Fletcher."

"No way!" Jacie's eyes opened wide.

"Get over it, Tyler," Solana said, pretending to be bored. "More amazing things have happened. Men have walked on the moon."

Jacie faced Solana. "Is this true?"

"Yeah, back in 1969 Neil Armstrong and—"

"Solana, you know what I mean."

"Yes, it's true," Solana said. "You should have seen Tyler." Solana edged extra close to Jacie and did an exaggerated imitation of Tyler staring at her.

Jacie laughed. "Well, I probably would have done the same thing if I'd been here. I thought the no-dating thing would last about a week."

"Well, when I make a commitment, I stick with it."

Tyler nudged them, pointing frantically at the court. "Look!"

Screams of "GO, KATIE!" surrounded them.

Katie Spencer stood face-to-face with Lakeview's star player, Ashley Jordan. Ashley dribbled the ball, moving from side to side as Katie attempted to get it away from her. In a flash Katie had the ball, and a groan of defeat filled Lakeview's side of the gym. Katie dribbled over to Stony Brook's end of the court and passed the ball to Becca, who swished it through the hoop for two points.

From that point on, the game was pure adrenaline. Defense was awesome, Katie made more amazing plays, and Becca scored two more times.

When the buzzer ended the game, Tyler, Jacie, and Solana leapt up, cheering with the other students. The band played as the group made their way down the bleachers to where Becca stood with the rest of the team.

"Great game!" Tyler said, punching Becca's arm.

"Thanks, Ty."

"You really gave Ashley Jordan a workout, Katie." Jacie patted Katie on the shoulder.

"She gave me one too," Katie said, wiping her dripping face with a towel.

Nate appeared and hugged Becca, lifting her off the ground. "Hey, Bec, you were awesome!"

I don't get Becca and Nate, Solana thought, unable to take her eyes off them. *They totally like each other, but they hardly ever go out just the two of them. How can they stand it?*

"Katie—you did great! I don't think Ashley will ever recover." Nate kept his hand resting on Becca's back.

Katie folded her arms. "Oh, she'll recover, just in time for me to kick her you-know-what the *next* time we're face-to-face."

Hannah appeared, camera slung over her shoulder. "I got some great shots of you two. Excellent game."

Solana felt energized by the game's intensity. "So what now? Let's go to the Copperchino or something."

"Yeah," Jacie said. "We can tell everyone about you and Tristan Fletcher."

"Tristan Fletcher?" Becca turned toward Solana.

"It's not what you think," Solana said.

"Well, I'd better hurry and go shower so I can hear all about it."

"You do that." Solana waved her hand in front of her nose. "You stink, woman."

"Thanks a lot."

"So, Hannah, can you come with us to Copperchino?" Tyler asked.

Hannah shook her head. "My parents told me to come home right after the game."

"Call them and ask," Jacie suggested. "We won't be late."

"Can't. I already missed family night as it is. I don't want to push it, especially since I got into trouble after the ski trip."

"You mean when you sneaked out of the house at midnight to meet a *boy?*" Solana teased. She still had a hard time picturing Hannah doing such a thing but secretly liked knowing she was capable of it. It made her seem more normal.

"Yes, ever since then." Hannah looked at Solana and put one hand on her hip. "Haven't you had enough fun torturing me with that?"

"No, I'll never stop having fun torturing you with that—at least until you do something more delinquent."

Hannah rolled her eyes. "Oh. So you need more material? Maybe I could start dealing drugs."

"Sure. Or start wearing a thong."

"Ewww!"

"Hey, baby, don't knock it until—"

"I'll do drugs before I wear a thong," Hannah interrupted.

"Drugs can kill," Becca added lightly.

Solana shook her head. "So can a bad thong."

● ● ●

"Don't forget, we want to be with you when you see how your project did," Becca told Solana when they ran into each other at the soda machine on Friday. "We'll meet you in front of the library as soon as lunch starts."

"Don't be late." Solana opened her soda. "Or I'll go in without you. I've been going crazy all morning."

"We'll be there."

As promised, Becca, Tyler, and Jacie were waiting at the library door when Solana arrived at lunchtime.

"Hannah will show up soon," Jacie said. "She said to go in without her. She went to get her camera and didn't want you to have to wait."

"That girl is so thoughtful," Solana said. She took a deep breath. "Thanks for being here."

"Are you kidding?" Tyler grabbed her by the arm and walked her toward the double doors. "The suspense is killing us, too."

Becca led the way into Stony Brook's library, which was unusually crowded for a Friday lunch period. Solana walked close behind her, acting as bold as always, like she couldn't care less whether her project came in first or fiftieth. She knew it was no secret to her friends how much she really cared, but she wanted to appear stone-faced to everyone else.

Solana glanced at some of the other projects as she moved through the clumps of kids gathered around displays. One student experimented with tooth decay—immersing teeth in cola, orange juice, and plain soda water. *Freshman*, Solana decided. *I did that experiment in sixth grade. The orange juice rots the tooth the fastest because of the acid.*

She rounded the next corner of displays, but still couldn't see hers because Becca and Tyler, walking in front of her, blocked her view. Her stomach fluttered.

"Solana, look!" Becca practically yelled. She pointed toward a long table next to the library's checkout desk. "You placed!"

Solana's heart pounded. She hurried to the table and saw a blue ribbon attached to her project. She put her hands over her mouth before a scream could escape.

Her friends yelled, "Yes!" at the same time.

Solana turned to her group, her whole face lit up with a huge grin. "I finally did it!" She turned back to her project. "I won!" she said, fingering the ribbon.

Jacie let out a squeal, moved around Becca, and grabbed Solana in a tight hug. "Solana, this is the best!"

"See, we knew it," Tyler said.

Becca and Tyler gathered around Solana and Jacie, trying to get their arms around them at the same time. A kid from Solana's science class walked by and called out, "Aw. Group hug!" They all laughed and hugged even tighter.

"This is too great," Solana said as her friends gradually let go of her. "I can't believe it!"

"Of course you can believe it," Becca said. "You only knocked yourself out for months."

Hannah appeared out of nowhere, smiling and reaching to hug Solana. "Congratulations, Solana. You deserve it after all your hard work."

Reaching into her book bag, Hannah pulled out a camera. "I'm supposed to take pictures of all the winners, especially first place. So, go stand by your project." Hannah held her hand out toward the table holding the winning entries. "Whenever you're ready, Solana."

Solana pretended to resist. "No, please, I'm a mess. I can't possibly be immortalized in the school newspaper looking like this. Where's my makeup artist? Jacie, come primp me."

Jacie reached over, adjusted Solana's hair, and pinched her cheeks. "There. You look lovely, darling."

"Okay, I suppose I'm ready." Solana struck a glamour pose. In a sultry voice she said, "I'm ready for my close-up, Miss Connor."

Hannah snapped several shots. "There," she said, smiling. "I'll make sure you get the first copy, Solana."

"And tonight we'll celebrate," Becca told the group.

Solana let her mouth drop open, feigning shock. "You mean *I* get to pick the pizza topping tonight? Oh, Becca, what an honor. I'm overwhelmed."

Jacie turned to Becca. "Does she get to pick the video, too? Maybe we should save something for when she wins district."

Becca laughed. "No, I think we should do something really special. We'll let Solana decide."

Solana looked at each of her friends. "I'll have to think of something crazy." She gasped. "I almost forgot. I need to find Dennis and tell him."

"I need to stay here and find the other winners to photograph," Hannah said.

"We'll meet you at the lunch table later," Tyler said.

Solana felt a hand on her shoulder. Turning around, she saw Cameron wearing his famous grin.

"I hear you're the big winner," he said. "Pretty impressive."

Oh, so he's actually speaking to me now. I'm touched. But Solana was in too good of a mood to give him a snotty response. She managed a smile and said a casual "Thanks."

Cameron stared at her like he wanted to say more, so Solana decided she'd better escape, quick. "Well, I gotta get going. My friends are waiting." She felt his eyes boring into her back as she slipped out the library door.

chapter 6

"I'm not wearing that. No way." Solana folded her arms across her chest, smashing one of the bright pink pom-poms on her clown suit. "I gave in to wearing a clown suit, blue frizzy hair, and hideous makeup. But *that* crosses the line." Solana plunked down on Manuel and Marciella's guest bed.

Becca held the bright red rubber nose out to Solana. "Aw, come on." Becca's own clown nose made everything she said come out in a nasal tone. "It's for Alvaro."

"You're not making Tyler wear a rubber nose. He isn't even dressing up."

"Actually he is dressing up. He promised to wear a cowboy hat."

Hannah stuck another hairpin into the edge of her orange wig to keep it from slipping. "This birthday party means so much to Alvaro. Why can't you just go with it?"

"I don't even like little kids."

"You like Alvaro, though—admit it." Becca held the nose closer to Solana. "Don't forget, you're the one who got on my case when I didn't want my parents to adopt him."

"And you're the one who *insisted* that we get Alvaro a piñata for his party," Hannah added. "As I recall, you even picked it out."

"You can't have a birthday party without a piñata." Solana snatched the nose out of Becca's hand. "Lucky for you I'm in a good mood after the science fair yesterday. Otherwise, this stupid-looking rubber ball would be flushed like a dead goldfish." She turned the ball around in her hands. "So how do you put this thing on, anyway?"

"Just fit it over the end of your nose." Becca took her nose off and demonstrated. "Squeeze it first to create some suction and *voilà!*"

Solana managed to attach her nose, then looked at Becca and Hannah. "Satisfied?"

Becca laughed. "Stunning. You should go to school like that."

Solana stuck out her tongue.

The bedroom door swung open and Jacie flew in, her dark curls still damp from her morning shower. "Sorry I'm late." She dropped her jacket on the quilt-covered bed. "Damien called."

Jacie grabbed the remaining clown suit hanging on the closet door and laid it on the bed. Solana, Becca, and Hannah watched her and waited, eager to hear the latest on the story between Jacie and Damien. "We talked for a long time. Too long, obviously."

Becca took a seat on the bed. Solana sat next to Becca. "What's up with that bad boy?"

"He's doing great." Jacie took off her shoes and tossed them aside. "He's getting really active in his church."

Solana shook her head. "Hard to picture a guy who drives a Harley and wears a leather jacket bragging about how active he's getting at church."

"Oh, stop." Jacie pulled off her sweater and turned her attention to Becca. "He's being discipled by one of the college guys."

"How exciting." Hannah took Jacie's suit off its hanger and started unbuttoning it for her. "I think that would be good for my brother Micah."

"What's the big deal about being discipled?" Solana asked, taking off her clown nose.

"Being discipled means having a spiritual mentor," Hannah explained. "It's a one-on-one relationship centered on prayer, Bible study, and accountability."

"Yeah, it sounds about as exciting as watching ice melt." Solana tossed her clown nose from one hand to the other, smirking at Hannah's enthusiasm.

Manuel and Maricella's doorbell interrupted, announcing the arrival of Becca's parents and Alvaro. Jacie gasped and scrambled to pull on her clown suit. "You all go ahead. I'll hurry up."

Becca, Hannah, and Solana hurried into the living room. Becca squatted down and held her arms out to Alvaro. "Hey, birthday boy!"

Alvaro stared at Becca and clung to Mrs. McKinnon's leg.

"It's me, Alvaro." She removed the fake nose. "Becca."

Mrs. McKinnon reached down and stroked Alvaro's back. "Sweetie, Becca and her friends are wearing costumes—like at Halloween."

Alvaro loosened his grip, never taking his eyes off his big sister. Slowly, he walked closer. When he recognized Becca, a smile lit up his thin face, and he started to giggle.

"Becca look funny." He lifted his eyes to Solana and Hannah, apparently trying to figure out who they were.

"That's Solana and Hannah," Becca told him. "Jacie's in the other room putting her costume on."

"Happy birthday, Alvaro," Hannah said sweetly. She squatted down next to Becca and stroked Alvaro's cheek.

Solana squeezed her rubber nose. "Honk, honk!"

Alvaro's giggle built into a full belly laugh. Becca bounced up and grabbed Alvaro's hand. "Come on, buddy. Let's go see the piñata that

Solana picked out for you. It's so cool."

Alvaro reached for the Cheerios box in Mrs. McKinnon's hand. "I'll hold this for you," she said.

Becca patted his head. "You won't need those. There's much better food than Cheerios at this party."

Solana and Hannah followed Becca and Alvaro to the enclosed back porch of the ranch house, which they had decorated in a cowboy theme. Outside, hanging from a beam, was a giant piñata shaped like a horse. Alvaro's eyes lit up when he saw it.

"There's really good candy inside it," Solana told him. "None of that cheap stuff."

Solana spotted in the corner of the porch the rented helium tank with several inflated balloons tied to it.

"I man the helium tank!" Solana said, running over to it.

"No, *I'll* do the balloons," Becca told her. "I don't want you teaching the kids how to suck the helium so they can sound like Donald Duck."

"What's wrong with that?"

"It might make them sick or something. So *I* do the balloons."

Solana snapped her fingers in defeat. "I'll be in charge of the horse rides then."

"Your uncle said Ramón would be in charge of the horse rides," Becca said.

Ramón? Solana made a face. *Since when is he part of this party?*

"You and Hannah are in charge of the games," Becca informed her.

"Do you actually expect me to play games with a bunch of human larvae?"

"No," Hannah said. "She expects you and me to play games with a few *children*. It'll be okay, Solana. I'll protect you."

"Ha-ha." Solana let out a phony laugh. "Okay, fine, I'll do the games. But no pin the tail on the donkey."

"We're not playing that stupid game," Becca said, letting go of Alvaro, who was already pulling away to get a closer look at his piñata. "We're playing pin the tail on the pony."

Slumping dramatically, Solana groaned and went back into the house, letting the screen door slam behind her.

Over the next few minutes Alvaro's friends arrived—two boys from his English as a second language class at school, a boy Alvaro had befriended at the hospital, and two boys from the McKinnons' neighborhood—a chubby blond named Justin and a skinny brown-haired older kid named Peter. Solana stood back, trying to figure out how six little boys could make so much noise. She watched as Alvaro transformed from his usual quiet self to a typical loud, screaming kid as soon as he joined his friends.

When Tyler arrived, Becca announced that the party had officially begun.

Hannah lined the boys up for the first game—a horseshoe toss using small plastic horseshoes. Solana stood near the pegs that the kids aimed for, while Jacie and Tyler stood on the sidelines cheering the kids on. The more she observed the boys' exuberance every time they hit their target, the more she found herself cheering with Jacie and Tyler.

She spotted Ramón by the corral wearing a cowboy hat and bandanna, brushing Carmen. Ramón lifted his head and tipped his hat at Solana like in the movies. She pretended not to notice. Ramón put down his brush, patted Carmen, and walked toward Solana.

"You know," he said when he reached her, "you look so familiar, I'm sure I know you." He looked more closely at her. "Oh, it's you, Solana. You look different today. Did you change your hair?"

Solana ran her fingers over the frizzy blue wig on her head and tried not to smile. "Yeah, that's it."

"There's something else, too." Ramón stuck his fingers into his belt loops and squinted. "You got a nose job!"

"Very funny." After grabbing three horseshoes off the ground and handing them to the next little boy in line, Solana asked Ramón, "Aren't you supposed to be getting Carmen ready?"

"Carmen can wait. I'd rather stand here and enjoy your new look."

"Yeah, the clown look is the trendiest thing right now."

"I noticed." Ramón nodded toward the others.

"Come on, boys," Hannah said, holding back her laughter. "Time for the next game."

Ramón bent down to the boys' level. "You having fun, cowboys?" He sounded like the host of a kids' television show.

"Yeah!" All the boys and Tyler shouted at once.

"You want to ride a horse?"

"Yeah!"

Alvaro and Peter jumped up and down, clapping.

"I'll finish getting Carmen ready for you so we can go for a ride!"

"It's about time," Solana said, a mock frown on her face.

"Oops. I think I'm in trouble." Ramón tipped his hat at the giggling kids. Before walking back to the horse corral, he winked at Solana and gave her the same boyish smile as on the day they met.

Hannah watched Ramón. "He seems nice."

Jacie walked over to Solana. "You should have made him stay."

"He has things to do—he's in charge of the horse ride," Solana said innocently. "Plus, he was getting the kids wound up. We can't let anything throw off Becca's schedule, can we? Now, come on. Let's play that pin the tail on the pony game!" Before having to answer any more questions about Ramón, Solana began herding the boys over to where Becca waited with the pony poster.

"Great job on the poster," Tyler said, patting Jacie on the back. "Too bad the kids are gonna stick tails all over it."

"Oh, I don't mind," Jacie told him, tipping her head back so it rested on his chest. She looked up at him and smiled. "That's what I drew it for." She moved to her post alongside the cartoon-like pony poster.

As Hannah lined the boys up, Tyler grabbed a tail out of Becca's hand. "Me first!"

She tried to grab the tail from Tyler, but he yanked his hand away. "Grow up, Tyler," Becca said. "This game's for the kids."

"So, I'm a big kid."

"He's too big," one of the little boys yelled.

"Oh, let him do it," Jacie said, laughing. "It'll be funny. Our own overgrown seven-year-old."

"Yeah!" Tyler grabbed the blindfold hanging over Becca's arm and handed it to Solana. "Tie this on me."

Solana took the blindfold and tied it around Tyler's eyes. She spun him around as fast as she could, three times to the right, then to the left. When she shoved him forward, Tyler staggered and groped at the air with his hands. The boys laughed loudly as he stumbled forward and pinned the tail on the back of Jacie's clown suit.

"Hey!" Jacie hollered. She shook with laughter along with everyone else.

Tyler pulled off the blindfold and looked around, pretending to be dumbfounded. With an exaggerated expression, he looked at where he'd fastened the tail. He gave a victory leap, yelling, "Bull's-eye!"

Jacie reached behind, took the tail off her back, and playfully smacked Tyler with it.

After that, not one tail got pinned on the poster. Following Tyler's example, the kids pinned their tails on Becca, Hannah, Solana, and each other.

Becca threw up her hands in exasperation. "See what you did?"

Tyler grinned. "Power, babe. It's all about power."

Becca rolled her eyes.

By the time the games ended, the kids were almost too wiggly to sit down for cake and ice cream.

"Whoever's quietest gets served first," Hannah promised as Becca's mother brought out a cake shaped like a cowboy boot and set it in front of Alvaro.

When every boy at the table quieted down and sat still in his chair, Solana turned to Hannah. "How did you do that?"

"Works every time with my little brothers and sisters."

Tyler stepped off the porch and yelled, "Ramón! Cake!"

Ramon joined them, and Jacie led everyone in singing "Happy Birthday." Ramón stood next to Solana, who only glanced at him before turning her attention back to the party.

A single candle shaped like a number seven rested in the middle of the cake. Alvaro watched it with a glint of fear in his eyes. Becca took his hand and whispered in his ear. Then they blew out the candle together. Everyone applauded Alvaro, who looked relieved to have the flame gone.

"I want a flower on my piece of cake," Tyler whined like a little girl.

"Me too," Ramón joined in. "A pink one."

Becca pointed to the cake. "Do you see any flowers on this cake? I think you're both hallucinating."

"Maybe the big boys need to eat in the kitchen," Hannah teased.

"Hey, yeah!" Tyler reached over and grabbed Ramón's arm. "Then we can have a cake fight and nobody will see."

They both ran toward the door. Peter jumped to follow. Becca pulled Tyler and Ramón back. "Oh, get back here. Some example you guys are."

Ramón flashed another boyish grin at Solana. She wished she could shake off the effect he was having on her.

In moments the cake and ice cream disappeared from the plates, and much of it ended up on the boys' hands and faces.

"Let's go ride, let's go ride," Peter started chanting, his fists rhythmically pounding the table.

"Let's go ride," the other boys joined in.

"Okay, okay!" Becca said, plugging her ears to shut out the racket.

"The boys who are quiet get to ride first," chimed in Hannah.

Silence fell over the little group. Becca smiled at Hannah. "Thank you," she said.

"You're very welcome."

Becca led the group to the horse corral, where Solana's uncle met them.

"You boys stay still and quiet now," Manuel instructed the eager group. "We don't want Carmen getting spooked."

Just in case, Becca, Hannah, Jacie, and Solana each chose a pint-sized buddy to stay close to.

"Are your hands sticky or anything?" Solana asked Justin before taking his hand.

Justin examined his hands, saw a frosting-covered fingertip, and lifted it to his mouth. Before Solana could stop him, he licked the finger and looked up at her proudly. "Not anymore."

Solana looked down at Justin. "That's gross, little man." She moved to the other side of him and took the unlicked hand in hers.

"Is that a real cowboy?" Justin asked, pointing at Ramón.

"He thinks he is."

Ramón smiled as he walked slowly toward Alvaro and held out his hand. "You first, big guy."

Becca nudged Alvaro toward Ramón.

Taking Alvaro's hand, Ramón walked him into the corral. Alvaro had been so excited about riding a real horse, but now he looked hesitant. The closer he got to Carmen, the slower his feet moved. He looked back at Becca as if waiting to be rescued.

"He'll be okay," Mrs. McKinnon whispered to Becca.

He's going to freak out, Solana thought, hoping he wouldn't.

Then she watched Ramón crouch down to Alvaro's level. "This is a nice horse," he said gently. He stood up and stroked Carmen's neck.

"See. She won't hurt you." Ramón picked Alvaro up and guided his hand to pet Carmen. "Tell you what," he suggested. "How about if your sister rides with you?"

Alvaro nodded, and Becca joined him in the corral. Becca mounted Carmen, then reached for Alvaro. After Ramón placed Alvaro on the horse, he took his cowboy hat off and put it on Alvaro's head. The hat almost covered his entire head. The fear melted away, replaced by a smile that started slowly, then took over Alvaro's face.

As Ramón led Carmen around the corral, Jacie whispered, "Ramón is so sweet."

"He's very sensitive with Alvaro," Hannah said, looking at Solana.

Solana shrugged. "I guess."

Jacie leaned toward Solana's ear. "Now, if you were going to go after another guy—which I'm not saying you should—but if you *were* going to, I'd pick that one." Jacie pointed to Ramón.

"Jacie, since when do I pick a guy because of his wonderful way with children?" Solana said, trying not to watch the gentle, confident way Ramón led Alvaro around the horse corral. "Besides, Carmen is probably smarter than he is."

I'm sure that's true, Solana thought. *It has to be true.*

chapter 7

On Wednesday morning, Solana met Becca and Jacie at their favorite table in the quad. Snow had fallen the night before, leaving a glittery dusting on the campus grounds. From the looks of the sky, Solana guessed that more snow would start falling any minute. Still, the three girls refused to move inside where they'd have to deal with the overly crowded halls that were so typical on cold days.

"Alvaro can't stop talking about his birthday party." Becca's eyes twinkled with excitement. "You should hear him going on and on—half in English, half in Spanish—about how funny we looked in our clown costumes, about the horses, and Ramón. He's Alvaro's new hero."

Solana released her hair from a scrunchie and started finger-combing it. "What does the kid see in him?"

"If you don't know, then you were blind on Saturday," Becca said, raising her eyebrows. "According to Alvaro, Ramón is *el vaquero* man."

"That's so cute," Jacie said. "It means 'cowboy man,' right?"

Becca nodded.

Solana snorted. "The *cowboy* man?" Once again she saw Ramón, tipping his cowboy hat at her, like he'd seen too many westerns.

"Yeah. It's *el vaquero* man this and *el vaquero* man that. Mom and Dad gave Alvaro a toy horse for his birthday. You know, the kind that looks like a broomstick with a horse head at one end? Well, anyway, Alvaro named his horse Ramón."

Solana murmured, "What a compliment."

"It is a compliment." Jacie kicked Solana under the table. "I bet Ramón would think it's sweet."

Solana kicked Jacie back. "I wasn't feeling bad for Ramón. I was feeling bad for the poor broomstick horse."

"Will you stop?" Becca said, folding her arms. "You're so mean."

"You are," Jacie agreed. "Ramón was great with the kids at the party."

"Next time I'm at the ranch, I'll let him know he has a fan club."

Solana felt someone tap her shoulder. "Hey, Solana."

She turned and looked up at Dennis. "What's up?"

"How's the science champ?" Dennis beamed. "I knew you'd win."

Solana smiled at him. "Oh, you're just biased."

"Okay, maybe I am a little." Dennis reached into his pocket and pulled out a computer disk. "I thought you'd better have this. It has all your charts from the project on it."

Solana reached for the disk. "Thanks. But I don't have the program that runs this."

Dennis shrugged. "It's your hard work, so you should have the disk."

At the sound of the bell, Solana and her friends stood up and grabbed their backpacks. "By the way," Solana told him, "I never could have won the science fair without all your help. *Gracias.*"

"No problem. It was fun, really." Dennis twisted one of the straps on his backpack as he walked. Solana caught him giving her one of those puppy dog looks that Jacie teased her about.

"So are you taking good care of your plants while they're here at school?" Dennis asked.

"Of course. I water them at lunch. Tomorrow I'm taking everything home, then it's off to Denver on Saturday for the district contest."

Jacie stepped up to the other side of Solana. "What will you win if you take first place there?"

"A top-notch telescope." Solana felt her stomach jump. She had wanted one like it since junior high. "The next step is the state contest, then nationals. That's where I could win a college scholarship."

"Wow," Becca said, turning around to walk backwards. "That would be incredible."

Solana nodded. The idea of a full scholarship to the college of her choice seemed like more than she should hope for, but she wanted it more than anything.

"I wish I could go with you," Dennis told Solana when they stopped at the door of the first period trig class they shared. They both waved at Becca and Jacie, who hurried down the hall to their own classes.

"Why can't you?" Solana asked. Had she said something to make him think she didn't want him to go with her? "You helped me so much. It's practically your project too."

Dennis held the classroom door open for Solana. "My parents are taking me out of school for a week. We're leaving today after third period to visit my grandparents in Southern California."

"Great," Solana said, dropping her backpack onto her desk. "Well, have fun."

Solana slid into her seat, then took her trig homework out of her backpack. *I guess it's better this way. Becca and Jacie would give me such a hard time if Dennis went.* Still, she felt a little disappointed. She really didn't want to go alone, and none of her *Brio* friends would be as interested.

● ● ●

That afternoon, Solana finished her chemistry test in half the allotted time. Glancing behind her, she spotted Hannah still working intensely. After reading over her own answers and finding nothing to change, Solana left her seat to drop her test in the box on Miss T's desk.

The teacher didn't appear surprised that Solana finished so quickly. Miss T whispered, "Here—look through this. You might find it interesting." She pushed a large book across her desk. Solana glanced at the title: *The Twentieth Century: One Hundred Years of Scientific Discovery.* Running her hand over the dust jacket, Solana turned to go back to her desk. Cameron looked up from his test paper, winked, and smiled at her.

Solana looked at Cameron out of the corner of her eye with an exaggerated look of confusion. Over the past week he'd gone from dirty stares to flirty smiles. She wanted to ask, "Why are you smiling at me? Do you have a split personality or what?"

Solana sat in her seat, shaking off the weirdness of it all. She opened the book, and her thoughts moved into some of the greatest scientific discoveries of the previous century. The bell ending class made her feel as if the power had gone out in the middle of a fascinating movie. She closed the book and returned it to her teacher.

On her way back, Cameron stopped her.

"How's it going, Solana?"

"Just *fabulous,*" Solana answered with all the sarcasm she could muster.

"I've been wanting to talk to you." Cameron moved closer to her as she reached for her backpack. He ignored the student behind Solana who obviously wanted to get by. "Why don't we start over? Will Saturday night work for you?"

"Are you serious?" Solana asked.

The students behind Cameron stood, riveted to the reality TV show playing out in front of them. Hannah gathered her books, her eyes fixed on Solana.

Cameron ran his hand through his hair and looked around at the curious classmates. "Yeah, I'm serious. Why wouldn't I be?"

"Oh, I don't know. Maybe because our last date was something I'd rather not remember. And maybe because afterward, you gave me looks that could kill."

Cameron chuckled. He shoved his hands deep into the pockets of his jeans and lightly kicked the floor. "I guess I've been a jerk. I was just mad about the way things turned out."

"I bet."

"So I want to make it up to you."

Solana smirked. "You don't need to make anything up to me. Forget it, it's over."

"Aw, come on, Solana. Can you at least think about it?"

This is getting pathetic. Feeling the stares of the students around her, Solana tried to think of a way to end the ordeal quickly.

"Hmm." Solana squinted, looked up at the ceiling, and pretended to think. "Okay, I've thought about it. No thanks."

Someone behind Solana cleared her throat. She turned her head and saw a tall girl named Madison. "Can I get through, please?" Madison asked, adjusting her backpack on her shoulder. "I need to get to drama practice."

Solana took Madison's arm and pulled her toward Cameron. "Maybe Madison will go out with you."

Madison curled her heavily glossed lips in disgust and scowled at both Solana and Cameron. "Uh, I don't *think* so." She shoved her way past Cameron and headed for the door while the rest of the class laughed.

Cameron's face turned several shades of deep red, and his eyes were full of fury.

"Excuse me," Solana said, attempting to push past Cameron.

He blocked her way, and the room became uncomfortably quiet. "You think you can make me look stupid, then walk out, *chica?*"

Solana's mouth dropped open. The nickname her friends used for her sounded derogatory coming from Cameron.

"Ooo, looks like I figured out how to shut you up." Cameron moved his face closer to Solana's.

"Move, Cameron," a guy behind Solana ordered.

Solana finally found her voice again. "Hey, you put me on the spot. Sorry, but you sorta set yourself up."

Miss T tapped on her coffee mug with a spoon. "Okay, I've heard enough. I'm pulling the plug on this soap opera right now. Now leave—all of you."

The group dispersed in a hum of groans.

Cameron stayed put, looking directly at Solana. He pointed a finger at her without saying a word. He backed up and headed for his desk, never taking his eyes off her.

Solana returned his icy expression and said nothing. She straightened her shoulders and headed for the door. Hannah ran up behind her. "Solana, how awful! I felt so sorry for you back there. I'm *so* glad you're not going out with him."

"I can't believe I even went out with him once." She glanced at Hannah, who looked like she wanted to say something else. "Don't *even* talk to me about the evils of dating."

Hannah put up her hand. "Don't worry, I wasn't going to. I was just about to say that I doubt anyone will go out with Cameron now. At least not anyone from chemistry class."

"Aw, poor baby."

A guy from Solana's trig class walked by and smiled at her. She waved back casually. *That's the third time this week that he's smiled at me. What's the deal?*

Hannah slowed down at the library. "Tell everyone I'll be at the quad in a few minutes. I need to renew a book."

"Sure, okay."

• • •

"You should have seen his face." Solana looked around the table and smiled proudly at her friends. "I wish I'd had a video camera."

"I wish you did too," Becca said.

Jacie set down her can of Coke. "Well, at least you won't have to worry about him asking you out again."

"That's for sure. But I don't get it. It's not like I've given him any signals that I'm still interested." Solana ran her fingers through the length of her hair. "That's not the only thing that's weird. Ever since I said I wouldn't date anymore, guys have been asking me out right and left. Tristan, Cameron, and a guy in my trig class who smiles at me all the time are only a few of them. Just yesterday I had three offers for dates. Can you believe that? You know how hard it is for me to turn down all that hot stuff?"

Tyler pressed his lips together tightly, trying to cover a smirk.

Solana stared up at him. "What?"

He shook his head. "You'll get mad."

Solana stood up. "I'll get more mad if you don't tell me."

Tyler took a deep breath, still smiling. "A bunch of guys have a bet going. 'Who can break Solana?' I think Tristan started it. He overheard you talking at lunch."

Solana slumped down. She eyed Jacie and Becca, who laughed along with Tyler. "Did you know about this?"

"No!" they insisted at the same time.

Becca turned to Tyler. "You guys are *awful*."

Tyler raised his hands. "Hey, I wasn't in on it."

"Maybe you should take it as a compliment," Jacie said, trying hard to catch her breath. "You're very popular."

Solana folded her arms across her chest. "A very popular *joke*."

Out of the corner of her eye she spotted Hannah, looking drawn and pale, moving quickly toward their table.

"What's wrong with her?" Becca asked. "Did Cameron ask her out too and scare the poor girl half to death?"

Tyler hopped up from his spot at the table and ran to meet Hannah. "What's wrong?"

Hannah ignored him, looking instead at Solana. "Something happened."

"What?" Panic filled Solana.

"I went to the library to renew that book and . . ." Hannah's hands fluttered helplessly in the air. "Your project—" Her voice broke. "It's—"

chapter 8

Solana sprinted to the library. Her heart raced. *My project! What about my project?* She yanked the library door open. Bursting inside, she wove through the displays, then stopped dead in her tracks.

"No." Solana could barely breathe. She slowly approached the table. Data charts and photographs lay shredded on the floor. One plant's roots reached into the air, its life-supporting soil scattered on the floor. Her sage plant had been completely brutalized—all the leaves pulled from its branches. Her blue ribbon hung proudly over the mess, as if mocking it.

She picked up one of the plants. As she gently cradled it, she smelled something that made her eyes water. She lifted it to her nose and sniffed the soil.

Bleach.

Solana grabbed each plant, one by one, and sniffed it. Every one had the same strong scent. The plants themselves looked fine, but she knew they wouldn't for long.

"Oh man," Tyler groaned behind her.

She spun around. All her friends stood there, their shocked faces mirroring her own.

Solana's throat tightened. Her eyes stung with the threat of tears. She swallowed hard. Jacie and Becca moved to stand on either side of her.

"Solana, what happened?" Becca said, barely above a whisper.

Jacie's eyes looked huge and stunned. "Who would do this?"

Hannah walked slowly over to the project and gently touched one of the plants. "Nobody was in here when I came in. Not the librarian or anyone."

Suddenly a short, thin girl emerged from the back room. A muscular kid followed close behind her.

"You need to be quiet," the girl said. "Students are coming in to study."

Feeling a tiny surge of hope that the two students might have seen something, Solana lunged toward them. "Did you see what happened to my project, Danielle?" She pointed to her ruined work. "It's totally trashed."

Both Danielle and the guy she stood with looked as shocked as everyone else. "I . . . I wasn't out here. I was talking to my boyfriend."

"Where's Miss Sparks?" Solana shouted, ignoring Danielle's warning about being quiet in the library.

"At a staff meeting." Danielle's voice lost all its confidence. "She left me in charge until she returned."

"So, while you were in charge, you went off to make out with your boyfriend so someone could trash my project?" Solana felt her voice starting to crack.

"No, I . . ."

I am not going to cry. Solana began to shake.

Becca rested a hand on Solana's shoulder. "Come on, Solana. We'll help you get this stuff home. It'll be okay. Maybe we can figure out a way to fix it."

"It can't be fixed." Solana couldn't take her eyes off the shredded data charts—the ones she'd created on Dennis's computer. He wouldn't be back until Sunday—the day *after* the district judging.

● ● ●

Jacie pulled her green Toyota Tercel into the driveway of Solana's parents' house. Solana slumped in the front passenger seat. Had this afternoon been real or only a bad dream? Bleach fumes hung in the air, leaving no doubt that Solana's nightmare was real.

"You guys don't have to help me transplant these," Solana said, still looking straight ahead, trying to think. "I can handle it."

"No, we want to help." Becca hopped out of the backseat, and Jacie popped open her trunk. Tyler pulled his car up behind Jacie's and got out, rushing to Becca's side to help her unload two bags of potting soil. Hannah and Jacie removed the brand new pots.

Solana got out of the car, cradling the remains of her backdrop. Her friends walked toward the house with armloads of pots and soil. They'd insisted on taking her to the plant store as soon as they heard her mention that transplanting was the only thing she could fix on the project. All four had pitched in to buy supplies.

"Too bad they didn't have any more sage plants," Hannah said. "Can you get by without it in your control group?"

"No." Solana shook her head wearily. "But Mama has a couple. When I bought my study plants in a flat of four, I gave her the two I didn't need."

Solana held the door open to let her friends in. "Bring everything to the back porch," she instructed. *Transplanting won't fix my project*, Solana thought to herself. *But I have to do all I can. No way will I give up.* Having the support of her friends had boosted her determination.

"Solana, what's this?" Mama stood in the hallway, watching the group with wide eyes.

Solana quickly told her mother what happened and asked for the sage plant. She fought hard to keep her anger under control.

"Oh, *mi'ja*," Mrs. Luz whispered, grabbing her daughter in a tight hug. She muttered sympathetic words in Spanish before letting go.

With the help of Mama and her friends, Solana had the plants in clean pots in less than half an hour. She stood back and took a deep breath. They all looked as good as new, including the plant that had been turned upside down. Solana felt her mother's arm around her. "Go sit down now, Solana. I'll make you and your friends something to eat."

"Sounds great," Tyler said, always eager for some of Mrs. Luz's cooking.

Solana shook her head. "You guys go ahead. I need to decide what to do next. I feel like going to Manuel's and taking a ride on Shadow. That's the only way I can really clear my head."

Mama Luz sighed deeply. "Okay, *mi'ja*. You go if it'll help."

"I'll give you a ride," Jacie told Solana. "I have to go to work."

"Thanks, Jace." Solana turned to the others. "Thanks so much for your help. You're great friends."

"Would we ever leave you stranded?" Becca asked.

"We enjoyed helping," Hannah said.

Tyler smiled at Solana. "When you win a Nobel prize, you can remember us in your acceptance speech."

"It's a deal." Solana followed Jacie to the door while Mrs. Luz ushered Becca, Tyler, and Hannah into the kitchen with a promise of homemade sopapillas.

● ● ●

"Thanks for the ride, Jacie."

"Are you sure you'll be okay? Maybe you should have stayed

home. I think your mom wanted to be there for you today."

"I know, but I don't want to be mothered right now. I need to think by myself."

Jacie smacked the steering wheel. "We should have reported this to the principal's office. They might be able to figure out who did it. Do you think it was someone who thought their project should have won?"

Solana shrugged. "Probably."

She felt bitterness rise in her throat. *Who would do something like this?* Her mind raced with possibilities. Anger boiled toward that nameless, faceless student.

At the ranch, Jacie gave Solana a quick hug. "Call me later."

"I will, thanks." Solana opened the passenger door.

As Jacie drove away, Solana turned toward her uncle's house. Shoving her hands deep into her pockets, Solana walked around to the back. *Is there anything else I can do?*

She began to make a list in her mind.

—I can take the film to get reprints of the photographs.

—I can reprint parts of the written report that I did on my computer at home.

But what about my charts? I can't afford to buy the program Dennis and I used.

A cold breeze blew Solana's hair into her face and she shoved it back. She dug into her pocket for a scrunchie and pulled her hair back into a lumpy ponytail. The closer she got to the stables, the faster she walked.

"Well, surprise, surprise." Ramón's voice caught Solana off guard. "You're just in time. I was about to muck out the stalls. Grab a pitchfork."

She scowled at him. *Does he ever go home?*

"I'm not here to help you," she grumbled. "I'm here to ride."

Ramón kicked the snow-covered dirt. "Too bad."

Keeping one eye on Ramón, Solana stomped past him into the stable. "I want to ride Shadow."

"Okay," Ramón said.

Seeing her favorite horse brought comfort to her heart—like seeing the right friend at the right time. She stroked Shadow's neck and mane. Tears stung her eyes. She scrunched her eyes shut until they ached. She put her head against Shadow's warm neck and wrapped her arm underneath it. "Shadow, you won't believe what happened," she told him softly. "I've never worked so long or so hard on a project before in my life. I was so proud of it. It was a winner, and now it's destroyed."

She sensed Ramón behind her. He cleared his throat.

Is he still here? Is he so clueless that he can't see I want to be left alone?

"Are you okay?" Ramón asked.

Solana took a deep breath and bit her lip to keep it from quivering. "I'm fine. Can you please get Shadow's saddle and halter for me?"

"You shouldn't ride alone if you're upset."

"Why? I do it all the time. I'm not six years old, you know."

"I know." Ramón walked slowly to a tall tack cupboard near the door. "Maybe it'll help to talk about what's bugging you first, though."

"I don't *want* to talk about it."

"Maybe I can help."

Solana turned to face him. "I seriously doubt it."

Ramón walked closer to Solana and sat on a stool. "I overheard what you told Shadow."

"You *listened* to me?"

"I'm really sorry. But since I already heard part of what happened, why don't you just unload the whole thing?"

"Why should I tell a rude, eavesdropping—"

"Give me a chance. Please?"

Solana considered a moment. Anger bubbled so strong within, she was going to explode if she didn't get it out. "Fine, I'll tell you." She took a deep breath and spilled the whole story. Ramón listened quietly until she finished.

"Wow." Ramón shook his head in disbelief. He looked up at Solana. "That's terrible. I'd be upset too."

"So maybe you can understand why I want to be alone." Shadow nuzzled the side of her head. Solana stroked him. "Now my chance at the district science competition is totally blown. I mean, I transplanted the plants, but I don't know what I'll do about the rest of it."

"All you have to do is reprint the report and the charts."

"Ramón, I did the charts on a computer program that my friend Dennis has. The guy follows me around nonstop for two-and-a-half years, and when I really need him, he's in California."

"What program did you use?" Ramón stood up.

She told him.

"Do you have the disk?"

"Yes."

Ramón smiled and raised his eyebrows. "We have that program on our computer at home."

Solana's jaw dropped. "You do?" She felt her hopelessness begin to lighten.

"Tell you what, let me talk to your uncle about what happened. I'm sure he'll let me leave. We can start right away."

chapter 9

Forty-five minutes later, Solana sat in front of Ramón's computer, which rested on a small pressed wood desk in a tiny bedroom of the apartment he and his mother shared. It didn't take long for Solana to retrieve her work. Seeing it on the screen felt like being united with a long-lost friend. While she set up to print, she noticed that Ramón was looking over her shoulder.

"Would you mind if I read your report?" he asked.

"I guess that would be okay." Solana clicked on "print." While she waited for the pages to emerge, she looked around Ramón's room. It was neat and simple but cramped with his bed, dresser, computer desk, and a large bookshelf, which held a portable stereo and was crammed with books. She squinted her eyes, wondering if she were imagining things. They looked like physics and astronomy texts, but she couldn't quite make out the titles. *Why would a ranch hand have books on physics?* She turned to face Ramón, who'd taken the first page out of the printer and was studying it. Solana watched him. On the drive over from Manuel's, he asked nonstop questions about her project, what the results of her study were, and whether or not her hypothesis matched the outcome.

"Why are you so interested in my work?" she asked.

"I've always been interested in studies involving the environment. I'm not at all surprised that you found a high acid content in some of the snowfall around here, considering the pollution level in Denver."

"You should see what acid precipitation did to my blue spruce over time. It developed a disease that made the needles fall off."

"And when they grew back, they were puny and fragile, right?"

"Right." The last data sheet slid onto the printer tray. "So, you know a lot about plants?"

Ramón sat at the edge of his bed. "I know a little. I've always been interested in all areas of scientific study." Solana tried to hide her shock but knew her attempt hadn't been successful when Ramón said, "And you thought I only knew about feeding horses and pitchin' hay."

Embarrassed, Solana tucked her hair behind her ear. All of a sudden she had a hard time looking at Ramón, knowing that she'd misjudged him—and that he knew it too. Once again she glanced at the bookshelf. *So those must be physics and astronomy books after all. He's probably read all of them.*

"You know," Ramón said as he removed the rest of Solana's pages from the printer, "just because a person works at a ranch doesn't mean that he has no brain." He held Solana's work out to her.

"Why *do* you work at the ranch?" she asked.

"Why do you help your uncle so often?"

Solana smiled. "Because I love horses."

Looking into Solana's eyes, Ramón smiled back at her. "Same here."

"Got it." Solana turned halfway around and closed down the file containing her data before removing the disk. "So, um, what are you studying?" *Somehow I have a feeling he won't say PE.*

"Well, I'm taking my general ed. classes now, along with some prerequisites for aerospace engineering. My goal is to transfer to either Cal Tech or MIT in two years."

I am such an idiot! He seemed so young, like he could still be in high school. "When did you graduate?"

"Last year. I graduated young because I skipped a grade in elementary school."

"How old are you?"

"Seventeen."

Solana swiveled the chair back and forth with her feet. So, this guy was smart, *really* smart! He was also a hard worker and—she had to admit—a really nice guy.

"Thanks for your help, Ramón," she told him. Feeling unusually self-conscious, she fanned the pages in her hands. "You saved my project."

"Glad I could help."

And I haven't even been considerate to him.

"Hey," Ramón said. "You want something to eat? I'm starving."

"Sure." Solana got up, suddenly aware of how hungry she was. She followed Ramón into the kitchen.

"My mom works swing shift, so she never gets home before midnight. She always leaves something in the fridge before she leaves. Nothing fancy, but it's always good."

"I'm not picky." Solana carefully laid her data sheets and report on the counter.

Ramón opened the refrigerator and studied its contents. "Aha! Homemade macaroni and cheese with diced ham, my favorite."

"As long as it doesn't have lima beans or red beets in it." Solana stuck out her tongue, then plopped in a kitchen chair.

"I'll eat anything that doesn't have broccoli in it. Mom tried calling them trees to get me to eat them as a kid. Didn't work."

"My mom told me that too! But she got frustrated when I asked if they were deciduous or evergreen."

"Well? Which are they?"

"Evergreen, of course!"

Ramón opened the microwave and stuck in the glass bowl of macaroni and cheese. "This'll take a few minutes."

He opened the refrigerator, took out two cans of root beer, and set one in front of Solana before sitting in the chair across from her. After opening his can, he raised it, like proposing a toast. "To whoever sabotaged your project."

"What?" Solana plunked her can down on the table.

"If it hadn't been for them, I wouldn't have had this opportunity to rescue you. How else would you have found out I'm not a moron?"

"Okay." Solana raised her can and lightly tapped Ramón's. "Nice to know my trauma was so fun for you."

Ramón laughed. He took a sip of his soda. "So, who's going with you to the university on Saturday?"

"I thought about asking one of my friends. I don't let my parents go anymore. Mama gets too nervous. Papa is loudly critical of the competition."

The microwave beeped, and Ramón got up to take out their dinner. "Would you mind if I went? You've got me hooked on your project."

Two days before, Solana would have scoffed at the idea. Today, she knew a whole new side of him—an intelligent side. Ramón would understand what she was talking about if she wanted to discuss other experiments at the competition. How could she say 'no' after all the time he'd taken to help her?

"Sure. You'd enjoy it more than my friends anyway." Solana said, looking into Ramón's deep brown eyes.

She got up from the table to help Ramón get their dinner. She noticed his eyes following every move she made and wondered, *Has he always looked at me this way?*

● ● ●

Becca ran up to Solana at her locker the next morning. "Solana, what happened last night? I tried calling and you weren't home. Are you okay?"

Solana shoved a book into her crowded locker. *I'll act casual for now, just for fun.* "I was busy fixing my project." She forced herself to keep a serious face.

"How?" Becca moved in closer.

Solana slammed her locker and spun the combination lock. A smile took over. "Becca, you won't believe it. Ramón had the program I needed to reprint my charts. He even took me to the store so I could replace the stuff I needed for a new backdrop. We went to a photo place and got reprints. The project's fixed, Becca. I was up until one in the morning, but it's fixed!"

Becca hugged Solana. "You're kidding! Oh, Solana, that's great!"

"What's great?" Solana heard Jacie's voice behind her and turned around to share the news.

Jacie's mouth fell open as Solana told her the story. "Really?"

"I'm just glad Ramón was at the ranch when I showed up. I never could have done it without him."

Becca leaned against the row of lockers, raising her eyebrows at Solana. "You sure have a different attitude toward Ramón now."

"Yeah," Jacie folded her arms across her chest. "Told you he was a nice guy."

"And he's smart, you guys. You'll die of shock when you hear this. He's majoring in aerospace engineering and wants to transfer to either Cal Tech or MIT."

"Whoa!" Jacie and Becca said together, looking at each other.

"How old is he?" Jacie asked.

"Seventeen," Solana told her. "And he's already in college."

"Sounds like he's brainier than you," Becca teased.

"Let's not go that far." Solana moved away from her locker. "He *is* a total science nut. He's going to go with me to Denver on Saturday."

Becca and Jacie looked at one another. She knew exactly what they were thinking.

"This doesn't count as a date. I just didn't want to go alone. Plus, he helped so much, I couldn't say 'no.' "

"Okay," Becca said, shaking a finger at Solana. "Just checking."

After swinging her backpack over her shoulder, Solana looked at her watch. "Well, I'd better get to the principal's office so I can report what happened to my project."

"See you at lunch," Becca called as Solana started off down the hall.

"And we're *so* happy for you," Jacie said. "I'll tell Tyler and Hannah."

Solana hurried toward the office. On her way, a familiar voice stopped her. "Hey, Solana." She turned and saw Cameron leaning against the wall. A mocking smile spread across his lips. "Too bad about your project."

She kept walking, then froze. *No one knew about this but Danielle . . . and that boyfriend of hers.* She slowly turned and glared at Cameron. "How do you know about that?"

Cameron paused a moment, something flickering in his eyes. Then he waved a hand in the air, trying to look casual. "You know. Here and there."

"*You* did it!" Solana said, her eyes blazing.

"Why, Solana, I can't believe you'd accuse me of such a thing." Cameron's voice dripped with sarcasm. "Especially considering our history together."

His cocky smile sickened her. “Don’t think you’re going to get away with it.”

“What? Are you gonna run to a teacher and tattle? No one would believe you anyway. You have no proof, and I . . .” he leaned against the hallway wall “. . . am a model student.”

“Before you get too cocky, your sabotage didn’t work. I saved the project, and it’s still going to the district competition.”

Cameron’s face darkened a bit, but he recovered quickly. “Good. I’m happy for you.”

“You’ll be even happier when I win,” Solana shot back.

“I won’t hold my breath,” he said.

“How unfortunate,” Solana replied. She’d had enough and was about ready to pound that arrogant smirk of his into the wall behind him. *Be cool, Sol*, she thought to herself. *Just be cool.* She turned and started to walk away.

“Solana,” he called after her, loud enough for the other students passing in the hall to hear. “Maybe it would help your chances if you showed a little leg. Wear something low-cut. That’s how you usually get what you want, isn’t it?”

Tears sprang into Solana’s eyes, and she felt her face flush warm. She gulped back a sob and glared back at him. “How would you know about getting what you want, Cameron? You certainly didn’t.”

chapter 10

JOURNAL

I don't get it. I'm more nervous about Ramón going with me to the science fair than I was the night of my disaster date with Cameron.

I've changed my clothes three times. I don't want to look like a nerd just because I'm into science. Okay, maybe I want to look good for Ramón, too. Wait, what am I saying? Why do I care what he thinks?

Solana had a hard time keeping still—if she wasn't nervous about being with Ramón, she was nervous about being with the smartest science students in the district. She'd calm herself about the competition, only to be sabotaged by thoughts of Ramón.

Who knows, maybe this is only the beginning of my science career.

Or maybe it's the beginning of—

Stop it!

• • •

Ramón led Solana through a maze of people and display tables in the gymnasium at the University of Denver. Solana's heart pounded harder with every competing project she saw. Each one in the room had won first place at an area high school. Many were so elaborate that they left her thinking, *A kid my age thought this up?*

None of the other projects at Stony Brook were anywhere near the caliber of the ones here. Is that the only reason I won? She bit her bottom lip hard. Then Jacie's comment came back to her: "People are always interested in studies that might affect where they live." Maybe she had a chance after all.

Since arriving shortly before one o'clock, she'd set up her project and explained her process and the results to the judges. While speaking to them, she felt confident about her study. Her mind was on her work, not anyone else's. Ramón stood by and listened. Now with her responsibilities behind her, she and Ramón were free to look around. For the first time, she stood face-to-face with the reality of her competition.

"Man," Solana said under her breath. "Look at some of this stuff. They make my project look so lame."

"They do not." Ramón turned around and gave Solana a reassuring smile. "I wouldn't have come if I thought your project was lame."

"Really?" Solana stopped.

Ramón took a step toward her. "Really." He smiled again.

Solana was taken back by how much his smile and soft eyes soothed her tension. "I was fine until I started looking around."

"Yours is great. You didn't try to think up the most outrageous experiment possible just to win. You studied something important to you."

Speechless, Solana could only nod. *How did he know?* As competitive as her friends said she could be, she hadn't tried to think up an experiment only to amaze the judges. To her, that wasn't science. Still, Solana couldn't help but wonder—would her acid rain study measure up? She took a deep breath.

Ramón patted her shoulder. "Tell you what," he said gently. "Why don't we get out of here—unless you need to stay longer?"

"Once I've explained my work, I'm free to leave. They send the results by mail. Oh, I do need to take the plants home."

"Well, you look like you need to get your mind off the competition for awhile."

"That would be nice." Solana looked down at her shoes, disappointed in herself for getting so freaked out by the other displays. Since when had a little competition gotten her down? Then again, she'd never made it to this level before. She'd only dreamed about it. She forced herself to think positively. *Ramón's been so nice. He's been patient all day. No way will I make him watch me pout.*

"You hungry?" Ramón asked.

"I'm starving."

"I heard someone talking about a great burger place near here. How about that?"

"That sounds great."

"Do you want to walk?"

"Okay," Solana said.

As Ramón and Solana searched for an exit that would point them toward the correct street, Solana spotted the domed observatory. She couldn't take her eyes off it. Ever since she was a little kid, she wanted to go inside and look through their giant refractor telescope.

"Have you ever been to that observatory?" Ramón asked.

Solana remembered how close she came to going inside only a couple of weeks before. *Should I tell him about the date with Cameron? No.*

That jerk is the last person I want to talk about when I'm enjoying myself. "No—but I've wanted to go."

"Would you like to go after we eat and gather your plants? We can hang around campus until it gets dark enough. We'll see what it feels like to be students here. You know, we can check out the bookstore, maybe sneak into a dorm or crash a frat party."

Solana laughed, imagining them bursting into a frat house full of unsuspecting jock-types. "I need to call my parents and tell them I'll be home later."

"That's fine because I need to call my mom."

"Let's do it then." Solana pushed the science fair out of her mind, determined to forget it and have fun.

They talked easily as they walked, and Solana wondered why she hadn't given him a chance to be her friend before. It seemed like only moments passed before they arrived at the popular hamburger joint. College kids with their faces buried in textbooks, as well as people Solana recognized from the science fair, filled the small round tables inside. Several groups spilled outside, where they sat on planters, leaned against lampposts, and sat along the curb.

The aroma of broiling hamburgers and sizzling fries made Solana's stomach growl. "I must have a bacon cheeseburger and curly fries," Solana said, digging through her purse for money.

Ramón put his hand on hers. "This is my treat."

"Thanks. That's really sweet."

"This way, you'll remember me when you become a famous scientist."

Wow, Solana thought as she made her way to a table for two tucked in a corner. *I could get used to this. He treats me like a lady*. While she waited, her eyes stayed fixed on Ramón. He looked so comfortable standing in the long line. Most guys she knew got mad if they had to wait behind more than two people. Ramón stood there relaxed, his hands in his pockets, talking to customers around him. Twice he looked over at Solana and smiled.

When he brought their food to the table, Ramón set Solana's in front of her before serving himself.

For the first few minutes they ate in silence. Then Ramón laid down his hamburger and let out a heavy sigh. "I'd better slow down." He squirted some ketchup into his paper dish of fries. "Are you feeling better now?"

Solana nodded as she wiped salt off her fingers with a napkin. "Yes, amazing what a gallon of grease will do for you."

Ramón leaned back in his chair and folded his arms across his chest. He reached for his soda and looked around the restaurant as he took a drink. "I like places like this. The hole-in-the-wall burger joints always have the best food."

"I know." Solana dragged a curly fry through the puddle of ketchup in her bowl.

"When I transfer to Cal Tech or MIT, maybe I'll work in a place like this."

"That would be fun." Honestly, Solana had always considered working in a burger place as the last thing she'd want to do. But today, watching the college students come and go, the idea seemed almost appealing.

"So, will you miss your mom when you transfer?" Solana took a sip of soda.

Ramón nodded. "Of course. I think it'll be harder on her, though. It's been just the two of us since my dad left. He moved to Texas when I was five." For a moment Ramón was quiet and Solana said nothing. "He remarried and has a whole new set of kids. So I don't hear from him much. About all he does is help pay for my college expenses."

Solana felt sad for Ramón. She couldn't imagine her own father divorcing Mama and going off to start a new family. And what good was money if you didn't get to spend time with your dad?

"What about your family?" Ramón asked. He popped his last bite of hamburger into his mouth.

"I'm the only kid at home now. My sister, Pilar, teaches fifth grade. She's really cool. My brother, Elío, lives in New Mexico and works for some of my dad's relatives. It's nothing that'll get him anywhere in life. He's kind of a flake—my example of how *not* to be."

Ramón laughed.

"I'm totally serious. Our parents have worked so hard to make sure our lives are better than theirs were as children in Mexico. Pilar and I work hard, but Elío has always been lazy. He wonders why people look down on him and won't hire him for good jobs. He says it's because he's Mexican. He loves to throw the discrimination thing around. I wish he'd see that it's because he's a lazy flake!" She noticed Ramón hadn't said a word. "That may sound mean, but it's the truth."

"It's okay. You're only being honest. Laziness bugs me, too."

Long after they finished eating, they continued to talk. Ramón asked about Becca, Tyler, Jacie, and Hannah, wanting to know all about them—how long they'd been friends, how they'd met, and what they were really like when they weren't wearing clown suits. By the time they walked outside, Ramón had also heard about Alyeria, their connection to *Brio* magazine, and the fact that although she didn't agree with her friends' beliefs, they still managed to remain inseparable.

Outside, the daylight had turned to dusk. *Have we really talked that long?* Solana thought. *It didn't seem like very long at all.*

"We'd better hurry and rescue your plants before they close the building," Ramón said, grabbing Solana's hand. His hand felt a little rough from working at the ranch, but his grip was gentle as his fingers wrapped around hers.

They hurried along the street and back up through the campus to the gym. There, they found a few people still lingering inside. Ramón helped her load the plants into two long boxes before lugging them to the car. The air had gotten colder, and Solana felt her hands growing stiff as they gripped the box.

"I have an extra pair of gloves on my dashboard," Ramón said before Solana even mentioned being cold. "They're those cheap, one-size-fits-all knit type, so they might not be *too* big."

"Good, I think I need them."

Ramón handed Solana a pair of blue stretchy gloves. As she put them on, she glanced at her watch and gasped. "It's almost seven and I never called my parents."

"Neither did I. We were having so much fun."

After they found a pay phone and made their calls, they browsed the bookstore's science section until the observatory opened.

Ramón took Solana's hand, leading her out of the bookstore. "The observatory's free. I've been here several times and always tell myself I need to come more often. Have you seen pictures of the huge telescope they have inside?"

"On the Internet." Solana's anticipation of finally seeing it in person spurred her to walk faster.

Inside, the telescope loomed high above them, more amazing than Solana had imagined. A man and two little boys were already at the top of the stairs that led to the viewing area, so Solana and Ramón waited at the bottom. Together they looked at the visible stars overhead.

"It's a perfect night for this," Ramón said. "The sky is totally clear."

"There's the Big Dipper," Solana said, pointing up with exaggerated excitement. "When I was like ten, my friends thought I was the smartest kid in the world because I could find the Big Dipper. So, of course, I went around trying to impress everyone with my amazing knowledge—even though I knew it was one of the easiest constellations to spot in the sky. But then my friends caught on and weren't impressed anymore."

“What did you do then?” Ramón asked.

“Learned to find the most difficult ones.”

“Of course.”

“My passion for astronomy was ignited then. I wanted to know all the stars and their names.”

Ramón pointed. “There’s Perseus,” he said.

Solana followed his finger to the grouping of stars. They took turns pointing out their favorite constellations—like Pegasus and Leo. Solana noticed that Ramón knew some that she didn’t. They became so caught up in their stargazing that they barely noticed others going ahead of them to the telescope.

Ramón slowly wrapped his arm around Solana’s shoulder. “This is nice,” he whispered.

She took her attention away from the stars and faced him. In the dark his eyes looked even more soulful. Without saying a word, Ramón leaned down and kissed Solana so tenderly that she felt her legs go weak. Solana kept her eyes closed even after Ramón pulled away. When she opened them, Ramón was smiling at her. He pointed to the couple at the telescope. “I guess we missed our turn.”

“So, we’ll wait a little longer,” Solana said. “That’s fine with me.”

Ramón looked again at the sky, but Solana didn’t hear the name of the constellation he was pointing out. Her mind was still in a daze from his kiss. No one had ever kissed her so sweetly.

When their turn came, she and Ramón climbed the steps together. Solana couldn’t wipe the smile off her face. *Nothing could make this night more perfect.*

“You look first,” Solana told Ramón, “then show me what you find.” She stood back as Ramón looked through the large lens and focused it.

“First, I have to find the moon,” Ramón said. “It’s a rule. You can’t look through a telescope without observing the moon.”

“Yeah, I saw a sign out front.” Solana moved closer to Ramón.

"They won't let you leave until you've seen it."

"And I think I just found the Copernicus Crater." Ramón stepped back so Solana could look at it. "At least I think that's it."

She sucked in her breath slowly as she focused in the lens. She'd seen craters on the moon hundreds of times with smaller telescopes. Through such a large one, the surface seemed so close and clear.

After seeing Mars, the cloudy atmosphere of Venus, and the rings of Saturn, they walked down the stairs hand in hand. *I have a feeling that the observatory wouldn't have been nearly as amazing with Cameron.*

● ● ●

In front of Solana's house, Ramón kissed her again—longer than before but just as tenderly. He squeezed her shoulder and looked into her eyes. "Let's do something like this again soon, okay?"

Solana nodded, her mind dizzy from his kiss. "Okay."

"Maybe we can ride Shadow and Carmen tomorrow."

"That would be great. I promised my uncle I'd give you a tour of the trails after I finished my project. Since it's finished, I guess it's time to keep my promise."

Ramón reached out and brushed Solana's hair away from her face. "I can hardly wait."

chapter 11

"Yo, Picasso, open up!" Solana drummed her fist on the locked door of Jacie's artist shack. She still felt super-charged from the night before. She felt giddy and unable to contain the extra energy.

If only last night could have gone on forever.

Even while she and Ramón were riding that morning, scenes from the previous evening danced through her mind—the long talks, browsing the bookstore, and mostly the observatory.

When she heard the lock click, Solana stepped back and rested one hand on her hip. She blew a giant bubble with her raspberry gum. The bubble popped the moment Jacie opened the door. While she peeled the remains of the burst bubble off her lips, Solana gave Jacie a phony annoyed look.

"Oh, I feel extremely welcome," Solana said, pretending to sound irritated. "You knew I was coming, but you locked the door? Some friend."

"Sorry." Jacie stepped aside so Solana could enter her small shack. "It's a habit, I guess."

Solana heaved a dramatic sigh and shook her head. "You know, paranoia is a serious problem. Maybe you need professional help."

Jacie pushed back a bunch of curls that had escaped her loose ponytail. "I don't want just anyone walking in while I'm painting or drawing, you know."

Hannah sat cross-legged on the floor near the space heater, looking through a stack of Jacie's paintings and sketches. Becca sat in Jacie's swivel rocker, flipping the pages of a drawing pad.

"*Hola*, ladies," Solana said, spreading her arms wide.

Becca and Hannah both mumbled, "Hi," with their eyes still buried in Jacie's artwork.

Solana turned to Jacie. "What are you guys doing?"

"We're trying to decide which pieces I should take with me." Jacie's eyes lit up at the mention of the upcoming art conference in Atlanta.

Solana looked around the small shack. As usual, none of Jacie's own work was displayed. "Oh, and if anyone should walk in through an unlocked door during the decision-making process, all would be lost! Like I said, paranoia."

Jacie swatted Solana on the arm. "Okay, so I'm paranoid. I admit it."

"Great. By the way, what's that guy doing out there with the binoculars?"

"What? Who?" Jacie ran to the window, then stopped abruptly. "Oh, very funny."

"You know I give you a hard time because I love you." Solana leaned up against the wall near Jacie's easel. "Can you give me a ride home later?" she asked.

"Sure. But didn't you ride your bike?"

"No, Ramón dropped me off. While you were all stuck in church this morning, we went for a Sunday morning horseback ride."

Hannah looked up from her stack of pictures. "I thought you didn't like him."

"Looks like she does now." Jacie leaned against the wall next to Solana. "How could she not like a guy who saved her science project?"

"How could I not like a guy who's also a genius and extremely cute and nice to me—all at the same time?"

"So much for kissing dating good-bye." Becca slumped her shoulders and swiveled Jacie's rocker with her feet.

Hannah shifted position, then adjusted her long black skirt. "Solana isn't actually *dating* Ramón. Are you, Solana? You said you'd given up on dating."

"I said I wouldn't date any more *boys*. Ramón is a *man*."

"Woo-hoo!" Jacie said, fanning herself.

"You get an 'A' in rationalizing," Hannah said.

"Here we go again," Becca groaned. "Now it'll be Ramón this and Ramón that—for about two weeks until someone better comes along. I should have known having the old Solana back was too good to last."

"Don't worry." Solana walked over to Becca and patted the top of her head like she'd pat a dog. "You won't lose me to Ramón. He's got school and a job. It's not like he's loaded with extra time to hang out with me."

"You must admit, Becca," Jacie said, "from what we saw of Ramón at the ranch, Solana just might be falling for a quality guy this time."

Becca nodded. "True."

"He took me to the observatory!" Solana said, pacing back and forth in the small room. "And Ramón acted like one of those people who leads tours in museums."

"A docent," Jacie informed her.

"Whatever. He knew everything about the different planets. He could find constellations that I've never found. I could have listened to him all night."

Hannah sighed dreamily. "Sounds wonderful."

"See? Even Hannah's jealous."

"But you haven't known Ramón for very long," Hannah said. "Be careful."

"Please don't get obsessed with him, okay?" Becca pleaded. "This isn't just about you not having time for us. It's about you taking things too fast."

"Becca does have a point." Jacie picked up a can of paintbrushes and ran her hand over the tops of the bristles. "Have fun getting to know him as a friend first. Damien and I have a deeper relationship now that we're just friends."

Solana studied Jacie's face and the reflective look that filled her dark eyes.

"Try dating the way Nate and I do," Becca said. "Bring Ramón along when we go out as a group. Then we can get to know him too."

"Group dating isn't exactly my style."

Hannah chuckled. "And look what problems your style of dating has brought you so far."

Solana folded her arms and scowled at Hannah. "Wouldn't you like to try my style of dating even one time, Hannah? Think about it, you and some guy who really likes you having dinner at a nice restaurant."

"Yeah, but look at your date with Cameron. I'd rather not go out at all than go out with guys like him. I like protecting myself from going on bad dates and making mistakes that I would regret later."

"Whatever happened to kids learning from their mistakes?"

Hannah looked into Solana's eyes. "Some mistakes have consequences that I'd rather not learn from."

Solana rolled her eyes.

"Just be careful, okay, Solana?" Jacie set down her can of brushes.

"Don't worry," Solana assured them. "I like Ramón a lot, but I won't do anything stupid. Anyway, I didn't come here to talk about my love life."

Solana grabbed the sketchbook off Becca's lap. "I thought we were deciding which masterpieces Jacie should take to the art conference."

Jacie unearthed a sketchbook from a pile of papers and began to slowly turn the pages. "I can't believe that in three weeks I'll actually be there! Can you imagine? An entire week surrounded by professional artists and people who love art!"

Solana flipped through another sketchbook, stopping at a pencil sketch of her *puros tesoros*. "This looks similar to the charcoal drawing that placed in the art show. Why don't you take that one, Jace?"

"You always want me to use those wild mustangs."

Becca stood up and looked over Solana's shoulder. "They *are* beautiful, Jacie."

They stood together staring at the picture. Solana tried to find some flaw, something to justify why Jacie always criticized her own work so much. As far as she could tell, Jacie drew like a professional.

"Have you seen those horses lately, Solana?" Becca asked.

Solana shook her head. "I don't see them near the trails much in winter. Plus, I got so busy with my science project that I didn't have time."

"When are you going to take us to see them again?" Becca stepped back. "It's been ages."

"Can we go when Jacie gets back from the conference?" Hannah asked. "I've never seen them."

Solana thought for a moment. "No, I think the next person I take to find them will definitely be Ramón."

chapter 12

Solana grabbed another handful of microwave popcorn. After munching a few kernels, she tried again to find something fascinating about the three poems in front of her. Mental film clips of the last two wonderful weeks with Ramón kept interfering—not that she was against those memories. It was just that she *had* to finish her homework. Mr. Garner expected everyone to be prepared to discuss what the poet wanted to communicate in each of the three works.

"Yeah, right. Like I can read a dead poet's mind. When will I ever use this stuff? I know, I bet I'll need to write poetry in the research lab.

"Oh, I finally got my wish,
Bacteria growing in a petri dish."

A knock on the bedroom door rescued Solana from her work.

"Solana," her father said as he opened the door and poked his head in, "the phone is for you."

As she took the cordless from him, he said, "It sounds like Ramón."

"*Gracias*, Papa," she said.

Her father closed the door, and Solana sat on the foot of her bed.

"Hello."

"Hi, Solana, it's Ramón."

Solana felt her stomach leap into her throat at the sound of his voice. She inched her way up to the head of the bed so she could lean up against the pillows and relax. "Oh, hi."

"I hope I'm not keeping you from anything."

"No! You rescued me. I was just doing my homework."

"Good. I've always wanted to be someone's hero." Ramón paused and took a deep breath. "You know, we've been having a lot of fun together—horseback riding and seeing movies and stuff. But I haven't taken you on a *real* date yet."

"Oh, really?" Solana teased. "You mean all this time I thought we were going on dates, we actually weren't? I feel so deceived."

"Well, so you won't feel deceived and I'll feel like I've taken you on a proper date, how about dinner tomorrow night at the Copper Mining Company?"

Solana's mouth fell open. She wanted to yell into the phone, "The Copper Mining Company? Do you know how expensive that place is?" Instead, she kept calm and said, "That sounds nice ."

"I hoped you'd say that because I already made reservations."

He's taking me to a place that requires reservations, and he actually thought to make them ahead of time. Is this guy for real?

"Should you ask your parents?"

Solana thought about how to answer. She'd dated since middle school, and her parents trusted her judgment. Lately, her version of asking their permission was to tell them where she was going, who she'd be with, and what time she'd get home. Of course, they always insisted on meeting the guy before she headed out the door. But they'd seen Ramón lots of times and always talked about what a "nice boy" he was.

"Oh, I'm sure it'll be no problem. They like you. If they say 'no' for some reason, I'll call."

"Then I'll pick you up around six, okay?"

"Okay."

After they said goodbye, Solana pushed the "off" button on the phone. She tossed it in the air. "YES!" She jumped on her bed, did the touchdown dance, and fell down, laughing, face first onto her bed.

"Solana?" Papa asked, poking his head inside her room. "Are you okay?"

She ran over, threw her arms around his neck, and kissed him soundly on the cheek. "Oh, yes, Papa! Ramón's taking me to the Copper Mining Company!"

"*Muy bueno.*" Mr. Luz patted Solana on the back, rescued the phone, and left his daughter to celebrate her upcoming date.

● ● ●

Making her way through the loud, crowded gym, Solana felt like she was floating. As she wove in and out of groups of students, she smiled and said, "Hi," to kids she'd normally ignore.

"Hey, girlfriends," Solana greeted Becca and Jacie. "Oh, and Tyler." She shoved her hands into the pockets of her jeans. She shifted her weight back and forth rapidly, unable to contain her excitement.

"Are you cold?" Jacie asked, watching Solana bounce.

"No," Solana said, her face feeling like one giant grin.

"What is your problem then?" Becca narrowed her eyes and looked at Solana.

"She looks like she has to go to the bathroom," Tyler said.

"I just have a lot of energy tonight."

"It looks like you've had too much caffeine or something," Jacie said.

Solana threw her arms up. "Am I allowed to be in a good mood?"

Jacie lifted an eyebrow. "Did Ramón call?"

Solana smiled and nodded.

"Did he ask you out again?" Jacie's eyes widened with anticipation.

"Yes!" Solana squealed, sounding like one of those perky girls she couldn't stand.

Tyler shook his head. "I don't get it, Sol. You act like Ramón's your first boyfriend or something. Every time his name comes up you're like, 'Oh, *Ramón.* He's so *amazing*. They should name a constellation after him!' "

"But he *is* amazing," Solana said.

"Of course he is," Tyler said. "Would you be bouncing off the walls if you didn't think so?"

Solana leaned against the bleachers in a dream state. "He's taking me to the Copper Mining Company tomorrow night."

"Wow," Jacie said. "I'm jealous."

"I'm not," Tyler said. "Ramón's an okay guy and all. But a romantic dinner with him—" Tyler shook his head.

"Oh, shush," Jacie said. She turned to Solana. "I expect a full report Sunday on the way to the airport."

"You'll hear every detail," Solana assured her. She thought about all the kisses she'd shared with Ramón and changed her mind. "Well, maybe not *every* detail."

● ● ●

From the window of Ramón's car, Solana spotted the lighted floor-to-ceiling windows of the three-story Copper Mining Company. A childish excitement came over her. The last time she was here had been the night of homecoming, with Derek Harris and all her friends. Tonight would be different. Tonight would be special.

"I've never been here," Ramón said, looking at the restaurant, which sat on a mountainside near Misty Falls. As usual, the falls were lit so people could watch them through the windows as they ate. "I'm glad I asked for a table by the window," Ramón said, parking his car. "The view looks incredible."

"You'll love the inside."

When Ramón got out of the car, Solana reached to unbuckle her seatbelt. Just as she placed her hand on the handle of the door, Ramón opened it for her.

"Thank you, sir," Solana said as she got out of the car.

Laying his hand gently on Solana's back, Ramón led her to a short line of people waiting for the four-person trolley that took customers up to the entrance. Solana noticed that despite the cold, some couples chose to walk up through the gardens.

"Have you ever ridden a real trolley, like in San Francisco?" Ramón asked.

"No, but I've always wanted to. Have you?"

"Umm-hmm. Mom and I went to San Francisco for a vacation once because her sister lives near there. It was fun. I have a feeling I'll like this trolley ride better, though."

"Why? I bet a real one is way better, especially in a big city like San Francisco."

Ramón smiled and grabbed Solana's hand. "Yeah, but *you'll* be on this one."

Solana smiled.

They stood still, just looking at each other.

The trolley operator cleared his throat. "Anytime you're ready."

They looked up to see the line had moved and it was their turn to get on. "Oh, sorry." Ramón got on first and kept hold of Solana's hand as she stepped on. They took their seats across from another couple. Solana figured they must be celebrating an anniversary or something because they kept kissing and snuggling with one another.

Solana and Ramón smirked as they pretended not stare.

As the trolley moved up the hill, Solana watched the gardens go by. Even in March the groundskeepers managed to make the dormant trees and bushes look pretty with colored lights.

The trolley stopped right in front of the steps that led to the restaurant entrance. As she followed Ramón, she thought, *I feel like I'm with an adult instead of a teenager*.

Once inside, Solana pointed out the real mining cars and rough stone cave-like walls. "And those are privacy booths," she told him, pointing to a row of booths enclosed with curtains. "They're for couples who want to be alone. The waiters knock before entering."

Ramón looked at her. "Are you serious?"

She and Ramón followed the host to the bottom floor, where he seated them by a window with a spectacular view of Misty Falls.

After the host handed them menus and filled their water glasses, Ramón leaned across the table to Solana. "This is better than I expected."

Solana watched him as he looked out the window, like a little kid who'd never seen a waterfall.

When Ramón started reading his menu, Solana picked up hers and tried not to look at the price side, but her eyes traveled in that direction involuntarily. *Can he really afford this?*

"I promise not to order anything too expensive," she said without thinking.

"Order what you want," Ramón said. "Between school and work, I don't have time to spend money on myself, so I can spend it all on my girlfriend."

Girlfriend? She gazed across the table at Ramón, loving the sound of that. "Okay. I'll have the lobster."

"You're worth it," he said.

I'm worth it? Solana thought as she propped up her menu. She allowed herself a moment to bathe in those incredible words before turning her attention back to the menu. No one had *ever* said anything like that to her before.

When the waiter came for the order, she decided on the chicken marsala—it wasn't too expensive, but not so cheap that Ramón would think she didn't believe him when he said price didn't matter.

After they ordered, Solana glanced at the other guests. Most were adults. She turned her attention back to Ramón. "I feel like we should talk about something mature—like current events or something."

Ramón looked around. "Me, too."

While they waited to be served, they talked about the same old stuff as usual, but it felt different in the restaurant's romantic atmosphere.

Their food arrived on the Copper Mining Company's dented metal plates with rustic utensils designed in wacky shapes.

Ramón held up his. "Did they give us the silverware that went down the garbage disposal?"

Solana laughed. "Yeah, in a nice place like this, you'd think they'd be able to replace the utensils once in awhile."

"Scenic view, cloth napkins, and dented plates with bent forks. Go figure."

Dinner flew by, and before they knew it, a brownie sundae sat in front of them, which they'd decided to share even though they were both pretty full after soup, salad, bread, and their entrees.

"We'll need to go to a gym and work out after this," Ramón said, wiping his mouth after a large bite of ice cream.

"Yeah," Solana said, discreetly licking some stray ice cream off her thumb.

"Can you do that in a nice restaurant?" Ramón teased.

"I don't care." She wiped her mouth and wiggled her eyebrows up and down, making Ramón laugh.

"That's one of the things I like about you. You're fun."

Solana leaned forward. "Only *one* of the things you like about me?"

"Aw, I could go on and on. But you'd get such a big head that I'd have to break up with you. And there's no way I want to do that."

Solana stopped, a spoonful of ice cream halfway to her mouth. With any other guy, Solana would have thought he was feeding her a line to get more out of her. But Ramón had only kissed her and treated her with respect.

Ramón sighed and stretched after the last spoonful of ice cream. "I'm never eating again."

Solana groaned. "Me neither. Everything was so good, though. Thank you."

"Thanks for saying 'yes.' " Ramón reached for Solana's hand, and they walked out of the restaurant. On the way out, Solana glanced at other couples. Some looked as happy as she felt, while others seemed uninterested. She felt Ramón squeezing her hand and thought, *Ramón and I will never have that bored look when we're together.*

"How about walking through the garden and up to the falls?" Ramón held the door open for Solana.

"Okay."

Outside, the air had grown colder, but Solana didn't care. She used it as an excuse to stand even closer to Ramón. When she did, he put his arm around her and they walked snuggled together through the garden. Solana hardly noticed the gardens. All she noticed was the warmth of Ramón's arm around her, the sound of his voice as he talked, and the starry sky above them. It reminded her of the night at the observatory when they kissed for the first time.

They found a path leading up to an overlook for Misty Falls and walked it without saying a word. Solana closed her eyes and listened to the rush of water that grew stronger with each step she and Ramón took. She opened her eyes when Ramón asked, "You aren't falling asleep on me, are you?"

"No," Solana said quietly.

"Good. I was afraid you'd gotten bored or something."

"I could never get bored with you." Solana immediately wanted to take her words back. *That sounded so cheesy.* She hoped Ramón didn't notice. But the words were true. Somewhere she'd heard that being in love makes you do crazy things. Maybe it also makes you say cheesy things you wouldn't normally say.

Ramón stopped when they reached the overlook. Misty Falls roared in front of them. He sucked in his breath. "I've never been this close to the falls before."

Solana looked around for other people. "And we're all alone up here. That practically never happens."

"Lucky us." Ramón wrapped both arms around Solana. She leaned her head against his chest. For a few minutes they just stood silently, watching the falls.

She remembered the day they met, when she'd snubbed him, and the day of Alvaro's party, when she'd been rude to him. "I can't believe we're even here together—I mean, after how I treated you when we first met."

"Oh, I knew that wasn't the real you."

"No, you don't understand. That *is* the real me."

"Yeah, but there's more to you than that. Knowing this side of you is worth all the effort it took to get here."

"Oh," Solana said, taking a step back. "Is that meant as a compliment?"

"Yes." Ramón smiled and drew her back to him. "It's a compliment."

He moved his hand to the back of her head and pulled her closer. Solana had no idea how long they stood kissing in front of the falls, but when they stopped, they were still alone. Looking up into Ramón's eyes, she thought, *I think I've found the right guy.*

chapter 13

"Jacie, how much stuff are you taking?" Tyler asked as he heaved a large suitcase-on-wheels into the trunk of his car. "Your suitcase is the size of my whole car." He slammed the trunk.

"I'm not taking that much," Jacie said. "I fit everything into one suitcase—except my portfolio, sketchbook, and art supplies. They're in my carry-on."

"Tyler, you know Jacie," Solana said. "She needs choices for what to wear so she can be creative."

Becca opened the back door. "Unlike you and me, Tyler, who throw on jeans and a sweatshirt and go."

"That's right." Jacie opened the front passenger door and hopped in.

"You're going to an art conference, Jacie," Tyler reminded her. "Not a fashion design conference."

"Still. I'll be with professional artists. I want to look *professional.*"

Tyler shook his head and got into the car.

Solana hopped into the backseat. "You two sound like an old married couple."

Jacie and Tyler looked at each other and laughed. "Yeah, right," Jacie said.

Hannah and Becca piled in beside Solana.

"Speaking of *couples*," Jacie turned to face Solana. "How was the big date last night?"

Solana sighed deeply, closing her eyes.

"I think the sigh-smile combo says it all," Tyler said, backing out of Jacie's driveway.

"It was the best night of my life," Solana said as the night's events flooded her with warm memories.

"I thought the night at the observatory was the best night of your life," Becca said.

"This was even better." Solana went on to describe every detail of the evening—including the kiss by Misty Falls. She loved it when Hannah blushed. "I guess I could have left *that* part out."

"Uh, let's talk about something else," Tyler suggested.

"Yes, please." Hannah leaned back. "We were talking about your kiss—I mean date, Solana."

"Well, *mis amigos*, I think I've found *the* guy."

Becca stared at Solana as if in shock. "You mean Ramón may last more than two weeks?"

"Hey," Jacie said. "He's already lasted almost *four*. Solana's going for a record."

Solana looked from one girl to the other. "I think I'll be with Ramón for a long, long time."

Hannah took a deep breath, then spoke. "Solana, I have to ask you this: When we all talked at lunch that day—you know when you said you wouldn't date anymore until you found the right guy—well, you said that when you *did* find the right guy you'd . . ."

Solana kept her eyes on Hannah, waiting for her to finish.

Hannah paused. Then her words tumbled out. "You said you'd sleep with him."

Solana smiled. Ramón's face flashed through her mind. "You never know. I might."

"Solana, you haven't been dating Ramón that long," Jacie said. "He's a nice guy—but slow down a little."

"There are some things that you just *know* are perfect," Solana said. "My parents knew after their first date that they'd get married. At the science fair I knew Ramón wouldn't be like the other guys I've gone out with. Last night settled it. He cares about me so much, and I care about him more than I ever have anyone else. If he asked me to sleep with him, I'd say 'yes' in a heartbeat."

"Listen to what you're saying." Becca turned to look Solana in the eyes. "You talk like it's no big deal."

"It *is* a big deal," Solana agreed. "I'm not saying it's going to happen. But if it does, I know it's going to be great because I waited for the right person."

"The point of waiting is not just to find the right person," Becca told her.

"I know, I know—according to your way of thinking, I'm supposed to wait for a husband." Solana folded her arms. "Why can't you guys let me make my own decisions and live the way I want to?"

"Because we don't want you to get hurt," Jacie said. "Remember when we made that promise at Alyeria? We promised to always want the best for each other."

How could Solana forget? In fourth grade they'd all met at their secret place, called Alyeria. It was a clearing in the middle of an aspen grove, near the playground of their elementary school. At that time, they promised to be friends forever. Then in eighth grade, they added a promise to always desire the best for each other. Becca, Tyler, and Jacie also promised to always encourage each other to grow in their relationship with God. Solana only agreed to encourage her friends to grow.

"Of course I remember," Solana said. She looked out of the corner of her eye at Hannah, noticing that she had that left-out look, as she always did when they talked about Alyeria—a world she'd never been part of. "But doesn't 'wanting the best for me' include wanting me to be happy? Ramón makes me really happy."

"It's great to know you've found a boyfriend who is good to you and makes you happy," Becca said. "And we all like Ramón—you know that. But we won't say we support you having sex with him because we don't. It's wrong."

Hannah spoke. "Don't you want to be a virgin on your wedding night?"

"That's not a big deal to me. What if I never get married?"

Becca groaned and covered her face with her hands. She let them fall into her lap. "You always have a comeback, don't you?"

"Always."

"Think about this, Solana," Jacie said. "Once you've given yourself away, you can never go back. Believe me, my mom has given me this lecture hundreds of times. You know, the 'I don't want you to make the same mistakes I made' speech?"

"It's more than just making a mistake," Hannah said. "We don't want you to get your heart broken."

"Ramón will never break my heart."

"Maybe not. But the consequences of your decision might."

Solana threw her hands up in frustration. "Let's drop it, okay? This is a subject we'll never agree on."

The next few minutes were uncomfortably quiet, except for Tyler's radio tuned to his favorite alternative rock station.

Solana looked out the window and thought about Ramón. *I wonder what he's doing now. Probably giving the horses their daily exercise. I hope he calls tonight. If he doesn't, I'll call him.*

Soon Tyler drove into the short-term parking lot at the airport. Jacie dug into the front pouch of her carry-on bag and handed Tyler some folded dollar bills. "Here, Tyler, it's from my mom. For parking." When Tyler tried to resist, she instructed, "Mom insisted. She felt really bad that she couldn't drive me herself."

Once parked, they all piled out of the car, stretching their arms and legs after the hour-long ride. Tyler removed Jacie's suitcase from the trunk, and they hurried toward the terminal.

"I have an hour and a half before my plane leaves," Jacie said, looking at her watch. "I hope that's enough time to make it through security."

"Are you nervous?" Becca asked.

"I'm excited about this week, but I'm so nervous at the same time."

"You'll be fine," Becca said.

"And you'll have a great time," Tyler added.

Hannah smiled. "You'll learn so much."

"But what if everyone there knows what they're doing except me? What if I'm the only beginner?"

"Relax." Tyler tugged on the strap of Jacie's carry-on bag. "You won't be the only beginner."

Jacie sighed. "I hope not."

"So then, what's your problem?" Solana playfully grabbed Jacie's arm and gave her a shake. "Go show them what art really is!"

"And remember," Becca said, "you're good enough to win the Copper Ridge Art Festival, so you're good enough for this conference."

Solana gave Becca a thumbs-up. "You tell her, coach."

"And God must want you to go for a reason," Hannah said. "Otherwise, you wouldn't have won the money."

Jacie puffed up her cheeks and blew out a long breath. "I'm trying to remember that."

While Jacie checked her bag, she started to bite her bottom lip and look unsettled.

Solana watched Jacie while Hannah's comment rang through her head. *Why does she give God credit for everything? And Jacie agreed with her. Jacie's the one who painted the winning entry, not God.* She looked at Hannah for a minute, then at Jacie. *It bugs me that Christians put God in the middle of everything that happens. God doesn't care that much.*

When Jacie returned to the group, her face was drawn.

"Don't worry," Solana told her. "Maybe the whole reason you're going is to paint a picture of Ramón for me. It'll become world famous and make millions of dollars."

That broke Jacie's solemn expression. She tipped her head back and laughed.

"Yeah, Sol," Becca said. "I'm sure that's the *only* reason Jacie's going."

When they reached the security gate, Jacie turned to her friends. "Well, I guess this is where we say good-bye."

"Have a great flight," Solana said. "Don't harass any flight attendants or anything."

"I'll miss you guys so much." Jacie chewed her lip again.

"You'll be too busy painting to miss us," Tyler assured her.

"We want to hear all about it when you get home," Hannah said. "And we'll be praying that you have a wonderful time."

Everyone hugged Jacie, then shouted and waved good-bye as she walked through the metal detector.

When Jacie grabbed her bag off the conveyer belt, Solana started waving wildly. "Call me as soon as you get there, honey!"

"Send a postcard!" Tyler yelled. "Oh, and don't forget to change your underwear!"

Becca called, "We love you!" and blew a kiss.

"Don't kiss any strange boys," Hannah shouted, laughing.

"Yeah," Solana called. "Bring them home for Hannah instead."

Hannah swatted Solana's arm.

Jacie turned around and blew a dramatic kiss back to her friends with both hands, spreading her arms wide. She smiled and shouted, "Alyeria!"

All but Hannah called back, "Alyeria!"

People around them stared. Jacie turned to Hannah. "We get those looks a lot. We just ignore them."

"I noticed."

"Come on," Becca said, putting one arm around Solana and the other around Hannah. "Let's go get hot chocolate or something."

"I don't want to get home too late," Solana said, wondering if Ramón had called.

"She wants to call *Ramón*," Tyler said, rolling the 'r.' He rubbed the top of Solana's head, messing up her hair.

"She has all spring break to call Ramón," Becca said, turning to Solana.

"That not the only reason I want to get home," Solana told her. "Pilar's coming home tonight to spend spring break with us. I haven't seen her in a long time."

"Excuses, excuses," Tyler teased.

"Okay," Becca said. "If we can't have you now, how about a hike on Monday? Tell you what—you can even bring Ramón."

Solana smiled. "That sounds great. We'll be there."

"At ten?"

"At ten," Solana agreed.

chapter 14

"Let's go in here." Solana gestured for Pilar to follow her into a discount leather shop at the outlet mall in Copper Ridge.

"Maybe they have some leather skirts on sale." Pilar walked ahead of Solana as both of them entered the store. "I've worn the one I bought last year so much that it's wearing out."

Solana spotted a clearance rack near the back of the store and made a beeline for it. The smell of leather filled her nostrils, making her want to buy something. However, finding an affordable item, even on the clearance rack, was probably a lost cause. But she still liked to look and imagine herself in one of the sleek skirts, jackets, or pairs of boots.

"So," Pilar said, moving aside hangers on the crowded rack to pull out a brown skirt. "Tell me more about Ramón. You two were on the phone for an hour last night. Mama says you've been spending a lot of time with him."

Solana smiled, thinking of Ramón. "You have to meet him, Pilar. He's intelligent *and* good-looking. I told you how he helped fix my science project."

Pilar nodded. "I've never seen you so excited about a guy." Pilar returned the skirt to the rack. "Your whole face lights up when you talk about him."

"Yeah, I know. Ramón has turned me into a total sap. I want to be with him all the time. Hearing his voice on the phone makes my heart jump up into my throat. I can't believe myself. Next thing you know I'll be wearing a heart-shaped locket around my neck with Ramón's picture in it. Shoot me if that happens." She leaned to whisper in Pilar's ear. "I think I'm officially in love."

"Is he a good kisser?"

"Oh, yeah! When I kiss him, I don't want to stop."

"So don't." Pilar shoved Solana's shoulder.

Maybe I can talk to Pilar about the "issue." She's slept with her steady boyfriends.

"Pilar." Solana lowered her voice. "How old were you when you . . ." She bobbed her head up and down slowly. "You know."

Pilar put the skirt in her hand back on the rack. "I was your age. Remember Tony?"

"You did it with *Tony?*" Solana wrinkled her nose. "That guy with the greasy hair and that stupid-looking wannabe mustache? Whatever possessed you?"

"Hey, I really loved him."

Solana snorted, trying hard not to laugh. "Does Mama know how far you went with him?"

"Are you kidding? Neither Mama nor Papa knows. And you'd better keep your mouth shut." Pilar looked into Solana's eyes. "Why are you suddenly interested in my private life? Are you and Ramón talking about it or something?"

"Well, it hasn't come up yet. But we like each other so much, I have a feeling it will. My friends lecture me about sex being wrong outside of marriage, but I don't agree. What do you think? Does it feel wrong to you that you sleep with guys when you aren't married?"

"No. It's not like I sleep with everyone I date." Pilar took Solana by her shoulders and looked into her eyes. "If you love Ramón and he feels the same way about you, then you should be able to express that to each other."

"That's what I think." Solana felt conspicuous in the crowded shop. She motioned to Pilar. "Come on, let's go somewhere else."

Outside the store they walked along the long row of storefronts.

"Do what feels right to you, Solana," Pilar told her. "Not what someone else tells you is right. As nice as they are, you don't always have to listen to your friends."

Solana nodded. "It helps to talk to you about this. You know, someone who understands my way of thinking."

"I'm your big sister; it's my job to give you advice about the *big* things in life." Pilar led Solana into another clothing store. "Are you and Ramón going out tonight?"

"Yes," Solana said. "We're going to Crazy Charlie's Fun Center to play air hockey. Real romantic, huh?"

"Sounds fun to me."

"That's the thing. We enjoy each other no matter what we do. Even if it's just working at the ranch."

"Looks like you found a keeper."

"I know I have."

• • •

Solana smacked the air hockey puck toward Ramón. He missed it.

"No! Not again." He groaned in defeat, watching the puck disappear down the slot. Solana raised both fists triumphantly into the air.

"Game over!" she shouted. "I win again!"

"I stink at this game." Ramón dropped his mallet on the air hockey table. "This is totally embarrassing."

"Aw, don't feel bad." Solana strolled over to Ramón's end of the table. She wrapped her arms around his neck and looked up at him. "I get a lot of practice at Becca's."

"Does Becca also have skeeball? 'Cause you killed me at that, too."

"I let you beat me at miniature golf."

"You did not. Don't mess with the one sport I'm halfway decent at."

"Uh, miniature golf does not qualify as a sport." Solana looked into Ramón's eyes, enjoying the fun of teasing him.

"It does too. I was in the miniature golf Olympics last year. Won a gold medal. Don't you read the paper?"

"So, that's where I've seen you before."

Ramón leaned down and gave her a kiss. It didn't matter that they stood in a room full of people—including little kids. To Solana, it was only herself and Ramón. That single kiss made her want to sink into the strong arms around her. Ramón gave her a soft look, took a lock of her hair, and began twisting it around his fingers.

"What do you say we find something I'm good at?" Ramón said. "Like ice cream."

Ramón took Solana's hand and guided her in the direction of a small kiosk where they both ordered chocolate cones.

"This has been really fun—despite my humiliation." Ramón rested his hand on top of Solana's. He licked a drip of ice cream off the edge of his cone. "Who cares that you made me look like a fool at almost every game we played."

Solana squeezed his hand. "I wish we could be together every day."

"Lucky you, you get your wish! Since it's spring break, we'll have lots of time together."

Solana took a couple of licks of her ice cream, never taking her eyes off the face she felt she could look at forever.

● ● ●

The week flew by. Every day, Solana and Ramón found ways to spend time together. Whether riding on the trails, playing in patches of snow, or working at Manuel's ranch, they talked, played, teased, and had a great time—more than Solana had ever experienced with a boy. Even tedious jobs at the ranch, like mucking out stalls and cleaning feeding troughs, seemed fun when she did them alongside Ramón. With Solana's help, Ramón always managed to finish his work early so they'd have time to do something else.

Thursday night, as Solana made her way up to her room to get cleaned up, she could still feel Ramón's kisses and his arms around her. During their afternoon ride, they had stopped for a rest and spent most of the time kissing. They had planned to go look for her *puros tesoros.* Instead, they got distracted with each other. That was when Ramón said the words Solana had only dreamed she'd hear a guy say to her, and then he asked the question she knew in her heart was coming. In the privacy of her bedroom, she let the scene replay in her mind.

"Solana," Ramón whispered after kissing her for who-knows-how-long. "I love you."

Just remembering caused her to melt inside.

"I love you too," she said in a voice that sounded strange somehow—like it belonged to someone else.

"I want to be able to show you," he said, his voice soft and tender. "I mean, I want to do more than kiss."

Solana didn't even try to play innocent and act like she didn't know what Ramón was talking about.

Before she could respond, he asked, "Have you ever?"

At that moment she couldn't have been happier to say she'd never slept with anyone. "No," she told him. "Have you?"

Ramón shook his head. "No."

Even more perfect.

"I've never dated a girl who means this much to me. I don't want to pressure you, though. If you're not ready, I'll understand."

"I don't feel pressured. I'm ready." She surprised herself with her sudden certainty. In that moment it was clear. She *was* ready. She looked up at him. "Because it's you."

A smile swept across his face.

"But," she said, "I don't want it to be a spur-of-the-moment thing. It needs to be special."

"Of course it does."

Ramón promised to plan the perfect day. Even that made her feel special. She'd never heard any girl at school say that her boyfriend took the time to thoroughly plan their first time together. That's because Ramón was different. Knowing he cared enough to make it memorable made the whole thing feel even more right.

Her mother's voice jolted Solana out of her daydream. When Mama opened the bedroom door, Solana pushed back her hair and cleared her throat, suddenly feeling self-conscious—as if her mother would be able to tell what she'd been thinking. "Hey, Mama," she said casually.

"Becca's on the phone." Mrs. Luz put her hand over the mouthpiece. "She's been calling all week."

"She has?"

"Haven't you gotten my messages?"

"What messages?"

Mama pointed to the desk where little white sticky notes lay in a stack.

"I never noticed," Solana said sheepishly. Then she gasped. "The hike! I totally forgot." She took the phone from her mother.

Solana's mother shook her head, muttering in Spanish as she

turned toward the door. "I think this boy is fogging your brain, Solana," she said before leaving the room.

Sitting on her bed, Solana turned her attention to Becca. "Sorry. I'm a flake. Go ahead and yell."

"You could have called." Becca was mad. "Tyler, Hannah, and I waited around for an hour."

"Hey, I didn't say for sure I'd be there."

"Yes, you did."

"Well, I—"

"Don't give me one of your lame excuses."

Solana lay back on her bed. "Okay. But when you're in love you'll understand."

"Excuse me, I think I need to go barf." Becca let out a huff. "We thought you must have been with Ramón."

"So, why'd you bother if you knew where I was?"

"To be polite. Not that you'd know anything about that." Becca paused. "I'm sorry. It's not just the hike. You haven't returned my calls all week. It's like you haven't had one moment for your friends."

"I've been with . . ."

Becca cut her off. "With Ramón. I know. I said you could bring him hiking with us."

"We like to be alone."

"Solana, you do this every time a guy comes along, only this time it's worse."

"Because Ramón's outstanding."

"Well, can you take a break from Mr. Outstanding and go to a movie with me or something tomorrow? It's only one afternoon."

Solana thought about it. Ramón had mentioned doing something special the next day. From the way Ramón had talked, she couldn't help but think he was planning their big night.

"Maybe," Solana finally told Becca. "I'll call you."

"Promise?"

"I *promise* I'll at least call."

"Jacie's coming home Saturday. You *are* coming with us to pick her up, right?"

"Of course. I wouldn't miss it." Solana smiled to herself. "I might have a lot to tell you on Saturday."

"What about?"

Solana thought about telling Becca and immediately decided against it. "You'll find out."

Becca growled. "Good-bye."

Right after Solana said good-bye to Becca, the phone rang again.

"Hi."

Solana grinned at the sound of Ramón's voice. "I miss you already."

"Really? Me, too."

If I saw this same conversation taking place in a movie or something, I'd make fun of it. What's happening to me?

"Okay, I thought of the perfect day. Tell me what you think. Tomorrow we go riding on the long trail—the one we never have time to take."

"That's where I see the *puros tesoros* most often. I can finally show them to you."

"Perfect! Then I'll drop you off at your house and you can get dressed up really nice and . . . well, after that, it's a surprise."

What could he be planning? Solana felt excitement build inside her. "What kind of surprise?"

"You'll see," Ramón said, sounding like he was talking to an overly anxious kid. "So, what do you think?"

Solana sighed, thinking about it. Everything sounded so romantic. "I love it."

chapter 15

I hope the puros tesoros *are near the trail today.* Solana rode Shadow ahead of Ramón and Carmen. "The trail we want is right beyond that cluster of pine trees," Solana said. She directed Shadow to slow his gait so she could ride side by side with Ramón.

Solana couldn't think of a day when she'd been happier. Even the weather seemed to have been planned just for her and Ramón. After a week of cold, the warmer air felt unseasonably pleasant. A light breeze blew Solana's hair back.

When they passed the cluster of pine trees, the trail veered off to the right, taking them to a place that always reminded Solana of being in another world. In this spot, with a thick grove of trees on one side of the trail and wide-open pastureland on the other, it was hard to believe civilization existed so close by.

"They should be around here somewhere." She rode ahead of

Ramón and gestured for him to follow. "I've tracked this group of wild mustangs for two years."

"That's a long time."

"I love my uncle's horses, but there's nothing as beautiful as the *puros tesoros*."

"How did you find them?"

"I found them accidentally while taking a ride by myself one day. I started following them whenever I could until I figured out their patterns—where they graze, when they have foals, stuff like that." She stopped Shadow. "Look. Over there."

Ramón stopped his horse beside her. At first they both sat silently, watching the wild horses in the open pasture as they grazed and galloped freely. Solana pointed out one black mare with a bulging belly. "That one's going to drop her foal pretty soon."

Ramón nodded, yet sat quietly for a few moments. Finally, he said in a soft voice, "Solana, they're amazing. I never would have guessed."

"Never would have guessed what?" Solana looked at Ramón.

"That you'd be showing me something like this. When you told me about them, I kind of got a picture in my head. But there's something different about actually seeing them. It helps me get to know *you* better." He turned to face her, then reached out and stroked her hair. "They're beautiful. Like you."

What do I say to that? She could only stare at him, unable to speak.

"So." Ramón maneuvered Carmen even closer to Shadow and reached out to take Solana's hand. "Do you show these horses to everyone you date?"

Solana shook her head and gazed out at a brown-and-white stallion. "No, only you. I've brought Becca, Tyler, and Jacie a few times." She looked at Ramón, wishing she were close enough to kiss him. "I show my *puros tesoros* only to people who will appreciate them."

"I do." Ramón took a long breath. "We'll have to come here more often."

"Yes, they can be *our* treasures."

"Let's stay and watch them for awhile longer," Ramón said. "We have plenty of time before we have to get ready for tonight." They dismounted and tied their horses to trees.

"I could stay here all day," Solana said.

They sat, their backs against a boulder, silently watching the horses. Solana's thoughts were anything but silent. The evening lay ahead, a huge unknown.

Am I really ready for this?

Of course I am. Why wouldn't I be?

But is he the right guy?

Absolutely.

How can I be sure?

He's mature, intelligent, he cares about me—he's everything I've ever wanted—and more.

Solana let Ramón hold her hand and play with her fingers. Her heart raced with her thoughts.

I'm so nervous.

What if he thinks I'm too fat?

What if he laughs at me?

Will I know what to do? Will I do it right? Maybe this isn't right. Maybe I should know more first.

Ramón leaned over and gave her a tiny, gentle kiss on the corner of her mouth and chased away all doubts. *At least for now.*

● ● ●

Ramón thinks I'm beautiful, Solana thought as she examined herself in the mirror. She smiled, turning to see how her dress looked in back. Other guys she'd dated had commented on her looks, but they'd never sounded sincere. Tonight, for the first time she felt truly beautiful.

As she thought how differently this date would end, she wondered, *Will I somehow look different after tonight?*

As excited as she was, she suddenly understood how Jacie felt before the art conference—excited but nervous at the same time. Her stomach fluttered, making her wonder—if dinner was part of Ramón's plan, would she be able to eat?

Her thoughts from earlier in the day replayed over and over in her mind. She pushed them away, pretending to be fine with it all.

What about getting pregnant? Becca's words of warning from so many weeks ago jumped in and set her off balance.

Well, Becca, she said forcefully to herself, *I covered that with two types of birth control. A girl can never be too careful.* Pilar had already slipped her a small bag containing several kinds the day before. Solana had quickly hidden the bag in a far corner of her closet where Mama would never find it. She hadn't told her sister that she and Ramón planned to do it tonight, only that they'd officially talked about wanting to sometime.

Solana took her bottle of Contradiction off the dresser and sprayed some on her wrists and neck. While checking herself in the mirror one more time, she heard the doorbell. She took a deep breath. *Are you sure you want to go through with this?*

Ten minutes later in Ramón's car, Solana knew she would go through with it. How could she back down now? Ramón appreciated her so much. He glanced her way often. "Wow, you look great. I love that dress on you. Is it new?"

"Sort of." She didn't tell him it was the dress she'd bought for the date with Cameron. Since she'd bought it for a night she expected to be special, she felt tonight fell under that category. Besides, she loved the way the tight-fitting dress made her look and feel.

Ramón drove into the hills, far away from the main road. *Where is he taking me?* Solana looked at Ramón, who gave her no clues.

"Close your eyes," Ramón instructed.

Solana obeyed. One scenario after another raced through her

head as she tried to guess Ramón's plan. She was scared, excited, apprehensive, and curious. Finally, he laid his hand gently on her shoulder. "Okay, now you can open them."

She opened her eyes and gasped at the sight of a glass-enclosed gazebo. The outside glowed with tiny white lights. Her mouth fell open. "I've never seen this place before. How did you find it?"

"I found it one day while I was hiking." He hopped out of the car and went around to Solana's door to open it. "I asked around and found the owner, who can't get up here anymore. In exchange for keeping it clean, he lets me use it anytime I want. I come here to study all the time. So I guess, for the evening, it's all ours."

Taking her hand, he led her up the steps and into the gazebo. A small space heater warmed the inside. A white linen-spread table was set with flowers and candles. Covered dishes sat elegantly on a hot tray in the center.

"You thought of everything," Solana said as Ramón lit the candles. "Did you cook this all yourself?"

"Not quite. A guy in one of my classes works for a caterer."

A thick mattress lay off to one side, covered in white sheets and a heavy comforter. Beside it was Ramón's portable stereo. Ramón pulled a chair out and gestured for Solana to sit. Before he sat down, he turned on an Andrea Bocelli CD and poured two glasses of sparkling cider.

"To the perfect night," he said, raising his glass.

Solana sat spellbound. As they sipped their cider and enjoyed the delicious dinner, she couldn't take her eyes off Ramón. The nervousness that she'd felt at home melted away with each moment. *I never imagined anything like this.*

Once they'd eaten, Ramón stood and held out his hand. "Shall we dance?" He faked a sophisticated British accent. Solana laughed as she stepped into his arms. Stopping only for an occasional kiss, they slow danced until the CD was over.

When the music ended, Ramón changed the CD. Elegant flute music filled the room. Solana closed her eyes, soaking it in.

She felt Ramón's hand on her shoulder, and she looked up at him. He held out his hand, and she put hers inside his.

He squeezed her hand, lifted it to his lips, and kissed it. "I want us to stay together for a long time."

"So do I."

He gently led her to the mattress. "Now, if you thought the observatory had a great view, wait 'til you see this." He touched her chin, causing her to look upward. She gasped. Clusters of stars sparkled through the glass, creating their own private observatory.

"Do you want to take advantage of the best reclining seat in the house?" Ramón offered.

Solana sat on the bed. Together they lay back and propped their heads up with pillows. They lay quietly for a few minutes, snuggling and gazing at the stars.

"Are you okay?" Ramón asked, smoothing his hand over Solana's hair. "I mean about what we planned?"

She looked at him and smiled. "Yes, I'm completely okay." *I think. I don't know. But you've done so much. How could I say 'no' now?*

He leaned over and kissed her gently. Solana felt herself melt, as she had the night in Denver when they watched the stars together for the first time. She rested her head against Ramón's chest and looked back up at the sky, waiting for the next kiss.

"I really do love you, Solana," he said.

"I love you, too."

chapter 16

Solana woke while it was still dark outside. Her own bedroom seemed foreign—almost as if she didn't belong. She knew where she belonged—waking in the gazebo, snuggling with Ramón.

As early as it was, she couldn't go back to sleep. She smiled and closed her eyes, remembering every moment of the time in the gazebo. Could the night have been more perfect? Ramón was so gentle and sensitive. Solana lay in bed for a long time dreaming about Ramón and what they did together. It almost didn't seem real. After all the movies, and all the talk, and all the speculation, it wasn't what she expected. It wasn't horrible. It just wasn't . . . well, she couldn't put her finger on it. But it felt like something was missing. Something very important.

As the sunlight filled her room, Solana sat up, stretched, and got out of bed. She caught a glimpse of herself in the full-length mirror and stopped. She studied her face, her eyes, and the way she walked as she stepped closer.

How odd. I look the same as I did yesterday. She turned as she did the night before, looking at her profile. First one side, then the other. Then straight on. Although she searched, she could see no difference on the outside. But it was as if she could see the difference inside.

Well, I am *different. I'm not a virgin anymore.* Right then, her stomach tightened and she felt her heart flutter. *But everything* is *right*, she told herself. *Last night* was *right. There's no reason to feel like this.* She shut her eyes tight and stepped away from the mirror.

Solana stepped into the steaming shower. She pumped gel onto a purple scrubbie. *What's wrong with me? I just experienced the most romantic night imaginable, and I'm not bursting with joy.*

Absently, she went through her shower routine, her thoughts crashing against each other. *I'm so fortunate! The most important event of my life has happened. It was perfect.*

Something's wrong.

Nothing's wrong. I don't need to wonder what sex is like anymore because I've done it. I'm happier than I've ever been in my life.

But I feel funny. Why? Ramón loves me. Our first time together was incredible. What more could I want?

She closed her eyes, tilting her face toward the spray. Water flowed over her face and into her ears.

Coffee. That's all I need. Coffee. I just didn't get enough sleep.

Downstairs in the kitchen, Pilar stood in her robe and slippers, sipping from a steaming mug.

"You were out late last night." Pilar sat at the table. "What were you and Ramón doing all that time?"

"Oh, you know," Solana said, trying to look casual. She poured herself a cup of coffee and sat at the table. "We had dinner, we talked a lot. Then . . . well, what do guys and girls usually do on dates?" Solana said quickly, trying to stall for thinking time. *Should I tell her?*

Pilar's dark eyes sparkled mischievously. "I don't know. What *do* they do, Solana?"

She thought of telling her, but couldn't risk her parents overhearing. So she just forced a smile. Looking at Pilar, Solana wondered if her sister woke up feeling different after her first time. *Yeah, it's probably part of the whole first experience. All new experiences feel weird.*

The sound of her parents talking on their way into the kitchen made Solana jump.

"Good morning, *mi'jas*," Mama said, kissing both of them on the tops of their heads. Papa came by and ruffled their hair.

"Did you have a nice evening, Solana?" Mama asked.

"It was wonderful!" Solana said.

"Tell us more," Mama said as she started breakfast.

"Did Ramón take you someplace nice again?" Solana's father asked. "Manuel must pay him well. Maybe I'll go work for my brother, too." He chuckled.

"Well it *was* nice, but not like a restaurant. Ramón took me to this incredible glass gazebo. He had dinner catered in. After dinner we watched the stars. It was really amazing." She hoped she sounded normal. She noticed Pilar eyeing her from across the table. *I bet Pilar knows,* Solana decided. *What about my parents? Can Mama see it in my eyes?*

"We must have Ramón over for dinner soon," Mama said, wiping tortilla flour off her hands.

"*Sí.*" Papa took a sip of coffee. "Since you spend so much time with him, we should get to know him more."

Ramón having dinner here*?* Maybe her parents would take one look at them together and know what they'd done. Papa would have a fit. The idea made her stomach jump.

The doorbell saved Solana from enduring any more of her parents' questions and Pilar's questioning looks. She jumped up. "Gotta go! I'm going with Becca and Tyler to pick up Jacie at the airport."

"Wait!" Mama called as Solana bolted out of the kitchen. "Take a tortilla."

Solana took the warm tortilla her mother held out to her. "Thanks." Grabbing her purse, she threw open the door. Becca stood outside, wearing a strained expression.

"Hi!" Becca said. "You ready?"

Solana almost asked her what was wrong. But she didn't feel she could deal with anything else. "Yeah, I'm ready. Let's go."

When they got to the car, Becca opened the passenger door and stood back. "So, you want to sit up front?" Her voice sounded flat.

Solana shrugged. "Well, if you insist." She slipped into the car.

Becca scowled as she got into the backseat.

"You can sit up here if you want, Becca."

"No. You always sit there."

"Oh, boy." Tyler groaned. He glanced over at Solana. "Hey, stranger."

"Hey." Solana smiled. "Where's Hannah?"

"We're picking her up next."

She stared at the tortilla in her hand. The inviting smell of Mama's cooking brought a lump to her throat and she couldn't understand why. "You want this?" She held it out to Tyler.

"Thanks." Tyler took it and bit off a big chunk. "Mmm."

Solana grew quiet, waiting for her friends to ask how her week had been, or if she and Ramón had done anything special in the last day or so. Her news about the night before didn't seem like something a person just blurts out.

"You missed a great hike to the falls," Tyler said with his mouth full.

"It was good?"

"The best hike of the year," Tyler said.

Hannah popped into the car, cheery. "Hi! I can't wait to see Jacie and hear all about the conference, can you?"

In response she got two half-hearted "yeah"s and a nod from Tyler.

"What's going on in here?"

"Nothing," Becca said, obviously irritated. "I just think it's too bad that Solana has missed a lot of fun stuff lately. Yesterday, Nate and I went to a movie with Tyler and Richard."

"I'm sorry," Solana said more quietly than usual. "I should have called." She felt sick. Her night was wonderful, but she hurt her best friend in the process.

"It's okay. I'm used to it."

"How've you been, Solana?" Hannah asked. "I've missed having you around. What fun things have you done this week?"

"It's been good. Riding horses and . . . and . . . stuff." Solana wanted to say more but certainly couldn't talk about the previous night with Hannah. Nor could she think of anything else to talk about.

A tense silence filled the car.

"What movie did you guys see?" Hannah asked Becca.

The three got involved in a discussion of current movies. Solana felt so out of it. They were the same people as always. But she had changed. Could they tell? Solana squirmed uncomfortably in her seat. Their conversation seemed shallow and almost childish.

At the airport, Becca hopped out of the car and took off for the terminal, not waiting for the others.

Hannah ran after her. "Wait a minute," she said. "We can't meet Jacie like this. Becca's obviously mad at Solana. Solana's acting . . . well . . . a little strange. We have to sort this out before it ruins the whole day."

Solana threw her hands up in the air. "What's strange about how I'm acting?"

Hannah looked at her and squinted, as if trying to see something in Solana's face. "I don't know, there's just something different. You're quieter than usual."

"That's a first," Becca snapped.

"I had a good time with Ramón this week," Solana said, her forced smiles beginning to feel normal. "A really good time. Especially last night. I was thinking about that."

"Fine," Becca said. "So you had a good time. But you ignored us all week long. We usually hang out together over school breaks, at least for part of the time. First you ditched us the day of the hike, then you said you'd call about going to a movie or something, and you didn't."

Solana felt like she'd been slugged, and rightly so. *But how do you choose between spending time with a best friend and a wonderful guy?* She didn't have an answer and stayed silent.

Tyler sighed and leaned against the car. Solana guessed from his expression that he'd already heard Becca complain.

Solana stepped closer to Becca and looked into her eyes. "I'm *sorry*, okay. What else do you want me to say?"

Becca folded her arms and pouted. "I don't know. That you'll start finding time for us instead of spending every second with Ramón. Having a boyfriend shouldn't mean that you dump your regular friends."

"I'm with you now." Solana widened her eyes and threw up her hands in exasperation, but inside, little guilt knives stabbed her everywhere. *Becca's right, but I'm right too.*

"Solana's got a good point." Tyler clapped his hands together and pulled away from the edge of his car. "She's here now, so let's not fight and ruin the time we do have together. So can we give it a rest? Becca, Solana's sorry. Solana, now you know that it really bugs Becca when you don't call. So make a bigger effort next time. Now let's go!"

"Jacie's plane probably landed already," Hannah said.

"Fine." Becca sighed and started walking toward the terminal. The rest of the group followed.

"Is everything okay now?" Hannah asked, looking intently at Solana's face, then at Becca.

"Yes," Becca and Solana said at the same time.

"You don't expect us to hug to make up or anything, do you?" Solana asked.

"No." Hannah giggled.

Becca turned around and made a face at Solana, and Solana made one back. Once again, that feeling of being different crept in. *I feel like I'm only pretending to act like the same old me. Why can't I just feel normal?*

Seeing Jacie's beaming face at the baggage claim perked everyone up. Jacie ran to Solana first and threw her arms around her.

"Solana, you were right. I did need to go to this conference." When she let go, she continued to bounce up and down. "It was the most amazing week of my entire life!"

Jacie grinned and gave each friend a hug. With her face still radiant, she reached into her carry-on and pulled out a plastic bag. "I brought you all presents." She handed a small floral-print notepad and a pencil to Hannah. "They're mini sketch pads, and the pencils are for drawing, but you can use them for whatever you want. All they sold was art stuff. I just had to get you something." She gave Becca a notepad with a cover that looked like denim. Solana's had a leopard print.

"Thank you, Jacie," everyone said together like a circle of kids in a preschool class.

"My way of saying I missed you." Jacie handed Tyler his gift, crumpled up the bag, and stuck it in her carry-on. "Even though I didn't want to come home."

"I think she had a good time," Tyler whispered loudly to Hannah as he waved his pencil and a notebook covered in music notes.

"I can't wait to tell you all about it."

"Like we'll even know what you're talking about," Solana teased.

Becca stuck her notebook and pencil into her coat pocket. "I want to hear every detail."

"So, let's go somewhere," Jacie said as she watched the baggage on the carousel move by.

"How about Sofa City Diner?" Tyler asked. "You know, that place where you sit on couches and eat off TV trays?"

"I love that place." Jacie spotted her suitcase and grabbed it off the conveyer belt.

"I've never heard of it," Hannah said.

"More proof you need to get out more." Solana nudged her.

From that moment until they were seated at Sofa City, Jacie told them about every minute of the conference—the classes she took, the people she met, and the professional artist named Athena who mentored her one-on-one.

"Athena is so awesome," Jacie said. "She told me my work has real potential. Can you believe it?"

"Of course we can believe it." Solana grabbed a menu. "We've only been telling you that since grammar school. But do you listen to us? *No!* You have to hear it from a professional."

"She also said, 'Jacie, it's so clear that your art flows right from your heart.' You guys, I almost cried. That was the biggest compliment ever. She promised to keep in touch by e-mail. And this summer Athena is doing an exhibit in Denver, so maybe you'll get to meet her."

"That would be great!" Hannah said. Her hand flew to her mouth. "Oh no! I forgot to call my parents. Tyler, is there a pay phone in here?"

"Over there." Tyler pointed toward a sign for restrooms and phones.

"Becca, can you order a grilled ham and cheese and a lemonade for me?"

"Sure." Becca nodded as she read the menu.

Hannah left the sofa and headed for the phone.

Jacie rested her arms on her TV tray and smiled at Solana. "So, what about you guys? I've been babbling so long, you're probably sick of the sound of my voice. I probably missed out on all kinds of stuff. Solana, are you still with Ramón? I mean, it *has* been a whole week."

Solana opened her mouth to answer, but Becca cut her off before anything came out.

"Oh, she's still with him all right. Every second of every day."

"I thought we were done with that," Tyler said, sending a warning look to Becca.

Becca looked over her menu and sighed. "We are."

Solana laid aside her menu. She looked across the room at Hannah, who was deep in conversation on the phone. *Now's my chance to tell them.* But she didn't know how to do it. They'd only say she'd done something wrong. Did she really want to hear that after such a perfect night? *They probably know it's coming. I wouldn't be able to hide it from them for long anyway.*

Solana smiled and flipped her hair over the back of her shoulders. "Let me put it this way, Jacie. Do I look any different to you?"

"Different how?" Jacie looked Solana over. "Oh, different because you are so gone on this guy? Well, sure, I guess."

"You're almost there. We are totally in love. And last night confirmed it."

Jacie cocked her head. "He told you he loves you already?"

Solana smiled even bigger. "Yes. Not only in words, but mostly in actions."

Jacie's mouth fell open. Becca and Tyler dropped their menus on the TV trays. Inside, she tried to figure out why her smiles kept feeling so fake. The tightness in her stomach and fluttering in her heart that she'd felt in the morning came back.

"Solana!" Jacie's eyes widened. "Do you mean?"

Solana only nodded, keeping her smile big.

Becca leaned forward. "*That's* why you were acting so weird in the car."

"Well, wouldn't you act weird?" Tyler asked.

For a moment Solana's three friends stared at her.

"It was so perfect," she told them. "Just like I've always imagined it would be. Even better!" *So why do I feel so strange inside?*

Before anyone could say anything else, Solana saw Hannah walking back to the table. She put her fingers over her lips and went back to reading her menu.

Hannah looked at everyone. "What's going on?"

"Nothing." Solana kept her eyes on her menu.

"You were talking about something. I saw you shush everyone up, Solana."

Deciding that it was better to tell Hannah part of the truth than nothing at all, she said, "I was telling everyone about my date with Ramón last night. I didn't think you'd be interested, that's all."

"So." Hannah sat back down. "Did you have a good time?"

Becca stared intently at Solana.

"Yes. It was *wonderful.*"

"All of it?" Jacie asked gently, sounding like there was more meaning behind her words. "Really?"

"Of course." Inside, Solana felt like she'd told a lie. She shook the feeling off and turned to Hannah. "Are you sure you won't reconsider courtship?"

Hannah laughed. "Maybe about the time you reconsider wearing mascara." She continued, "The more I watch you, the more convinced I am to stick with it."

"Good!" Becca said firmly as a waitress walked over. "Don't ever take Solana's advice when it comes to guys."

After they ordered, Solana found it hard to keep up her glowing, "last night was so perfect" routine. When she talked, she babbled about stupid things. Her friends didn't seem to know what to talk about either, as if hearing Solana's latest news made it impossible to talk about ordinary things. Solana couldn't finish her lunch. What little she ate sat like a rock in her stomach. Each time she took a bite, she felt three pairs of eyes digging into her, like they expected her to eat differently now. She couldn't wait to go home.

On the ride back to Copper Ridge, she was thankful she didn't have to talk. Jacie continued to fill them in about the conference.

When Tyler dropped off Solana, Jacie got out to say goodbye. "See you at school." She leaned in and whispered, "If you want to talk, call me."

Solana nodded. "Thanks. See you Monday."

Watching her friends drive off gave Solana an odd feeling in her heart. She realized she now had to face something that she didn't want to face.

She opened the door to an empty house and a note on the counter. "Went to a movie—will be home for dinner. Call Ramón."

Her stomach churned worse as she picked up the phone. *Maybe I'll feel better after I talk to him.*

Instead, the sound of his voice made her feel exposed.

"How are you?" Ramón asked.

Solana forced herself to sound cheerful. "Good." *Does he feel the same way I do? Should I ask? No, I don't want him to think I regret what we did. Maybe I do—do I?*

"Last night was . . ." Ramón paused and lowered his voice. "Great."

"I know." *Think about that. Just concentrate on how perfect everything was.*

"I missed you today," Ramón said.

"I missed you too." *So why do I want an excuse to get off the phone?*

"Let's do something tomorrow. Come by the ranch."

Her mixed-up feelings made Solana not want to see him. What if he caught on?

"Actually, Pilar's leaving tomorrow. I kind of feel like I should be here."

"Oh." Ramón sounded disappointed, which made Solana feel even worse. "Are you sure everything's okay?" he asked. "You sound kind of funny."

"Everything's fine."

"Call me tomorrow after your sister leaves. Okay?"

"Okay."

She hung up feeling odd. She felt so close to Ramón that a part of her wanted to pull away as if she were suffocating. She dreaded the return of her parents and Pilar. She just wanted to be alone.

chapter 17

The next day, Pilar took a final look around her room before closing her suitcase. "Are you doing something with Ramón today?"

Solana shook her head. She swallowed back tears. "No." She'd expected the heaviness in her heart to be better today. Instead, it felt worse. During the night she'd dreamed about Ramón.

Pilar sat down on the bed beside Solana. "Hey, what's bothering you? Did you and Ramón have a fight?"

"No." She took a deep breath, twisting a strand of hair around her fingers. *Maybe talking to Pilar would help. She should know how to get me out of this funk.* "You know when I told you that Ramón and I talked about . . ." She couldn't even say the word. What was she supposed to call it now that she'd actually done it? All the words she'd used before seemed so casual and empty for describing something so personal and intense.

Pilar smiled. "I know what you're talking about."

"Well, on Friday night in the gazebo . . ."

Pilar bounced on the bed and screeched. "I knew it!" She grabbed Solana's hands. "So, how was it?"

"It was great," Solana said half heartedly. She felt tears welling up in her eyes. Why was her sister reacting as if she'd been invited to the prom or gotten into the college of her choice? Couldn't she see the hurt on her face? "At least at the time it was great. Well, I mean, the leading up to it was great, the closeness was amazing. But the sex itself was so disappointing. I expected so much more. Now I feel, I don't know how to explain it. I feel bad inside, like something's wrong."

She waited for her sister to reach out and hug her and say some words of comfort. Instead, Pilar laughed. "Of course it was disappointing. The first time usually is. But you have to start somewhere. It gets better the more you do it. And the fact that part of it was great means you've started out well. A lot of girls can't look back on their first time and say that, you know."

A tear trickled down Solana's cheek and she brushed it away, choking back the rest. "I don't know. Did you feel bad after your first time with Tony?"

Pilar looked up at the ceiling. "I guess. Maybe at first. I remember feeling guilty at mass the next day. I even went to another parish to confess because I was afraid our priest would tell on me." Pilar patted Solana's leg. "But I got over all that. So will you. Don't worry. The first time is always a little rough. It'll get better."

Solana traced the patchwork pattern on the bedspread with her finger. Pilar made it sound so easy. Even when she gave her the bag of birth control, she did it with a conspiratorial smile on her face. Why didn't Pilar warn her about what the day after might feel like? Maybe she'd call one of her friends later to talk. Jacie said to call if she needed to talk. No, she'd probably just give her the I-told-you-so speech.

"Well." Pilar hopped up from the bed and grabbed her suitcase.

"I need to get going. And don't worry. You'll be okay."

"I guess," Solana whispered before standing up and following her sister to the door.

In the entryway Mama kissed Pilar on the cheek. "Call when you get there."

"I will, Mama."

"And teach those kids a lot this week," Papa added.

After hugging her parents goodbye, Pilar turned to Solana. "Hold onto Ramón." She winked at Solana before giving her a tight hug. "You don't want to lose him. And have *lots* of fun."

"I will," she said, trying hard to sound lighthearted. Pilar's words made Solana's heart thump.

Solana watched Pilar drive away before going back into the house. Pilar's words echoed in her ears: "Hold onto Ramón." Did she mean Solana might lose him if she admitted her feelings? She couldn't afford to risk that.

In the family room she flopped down on the couch and picked up the remote control.

Mama walked over and looked down at her. "You okay?" She laid her hand on Solana's forehead, then felt her cheeks. "Are you sick?"

Solana shook her head. "I'm tired."

"She's had too many late nights with Ramón," Papa said as he walked by on his way to the garage.

"I just need to veg out for awhile."

"Okay." Solana's mother stroked her hair before leaving the room.

Maybe I'll feel better if I call Ramón. Maybe I just miss him.

● ● ●

"I'm glad you called," Ramón said, leaning over and kissing Solana. She had hardly said anything on the ride home from Ramón's apartment. Silently, she was trying to figure what had gone wrong *this* time.

She went to the ranch at five o'clock, just like Ramón suggested, hoping they'd go for a ride. Instead, he wanted to get a pizza and go to his place. The evening ended in his bedroom. This time proved far less romantic than the first. All the way home, Solana tried to snap herself out of the deep disappointment she felt. She couldn't expect every time with Ramón to be as memorable as that first night. But would every date end the same way from now on? What about having fun together? What about kissing a little and that's it—like the night at Crazy Charlie's? Was that possible now?

"You okay?" Ramón asked, searching Solana's eyes.

"Yeah," she whispered. "I have a lot of homework." She desperately wanted to tell Ramón how she felt. Maybe he'd hold her and say he felt the same way. Maybe he wanted to go back to the way things were before Friday night. Then again, what if he didn't? What if telling him how confused she felt made him mad and he broke up with her? Looking into his eyes, she forced a smile and gave him one more kiss. *I don't want to lose him. I'm sure I'll feel better soon. Our relationship has moved to a deeper level, and I need to get used to it.*

● ● ●

Thursday night at the basketball game, Solana tried to keep her mind focused on the plays but kept disappearing into her own world.

"Solana, are you awake?" Jacie tapped Solana's arm. "You're off in space somewhere. Did you even see that basket Becca made?"

"I saw it," Solana said. She just didn't feel like jumping up and cheering for Becca like everyone else. Since the beginning of the game she'd gone through the motions of clapping every time Stony Brook scored, yelling to Becca when it looked like she might be on her way to helping the team, and laughing with Jacie, Tyler, Nate, and Hannah. But it all felt unreal and forced.

She'd been with Ramón again on Tuesday. That day they went to Solana's room while her father was working and Mama did the shopping. Solana almost asked Ramón if they could just kiss or snuggle and talk like they used to. One long touch from Ramón changed her mind. It felt good to have him kiss her and hold her. She didn't want that to end. Out of the corner of her eye, Solana watched Jacie and Tyler. Jacie took a bag of red licorice out of her over stuffed purse and passed it down the row to Tyler, Nate, and Hannah. Tyler bit the ends off his piece of licorice and blew through it, sending a thin gust of air into Jacie's hair.

"Hey." Jacie whacked Tyler with a piece of licorice.

Tyler looked at her innocently. "What?"

Jacie shoved him and laughed. "You know what, you brat."

When Jacie turned toward Solana, Tyler blew again, and Nate joined in. Jacie ignored them, smoothed out her hair, and held the bag out to Solana. "Want one?"

"Thanks." Solana took a long red stick out of the bag. As she chewed it slowly, she kept one eye on her friends. Tyler and Nate were putting chunks of licorice on their front teeth and smiling at Hannah, who smirked at first then burst out laughing when Tyler started singing an off-key version of "All I Want for Christmas Is My Two Front Teeth." Usually, Solana would have thought up something even sillier. She wanted to. But she couldn't even find a laugh to join Hannah's.

Her heart ached with envy. She wished she could act crazy and immature with her friends again. A part of her felt more grown-up now—like she'd matured ten years in a week. She felt the same way she did that time when she was seven years old and Mama took her to the playground. Right away, she ran for her favorite equipment—a small merry-go-round with four horses attached. As soon as she climbed on, her knees hit the handlebars.

Mama walked her all around the playground, coaxing her to try other equipment. But nothing else seemed as fun, so she moped all morning, wishing she could shrink small enough to ride those horses again.

Now, sitting with her friends, all she wanted to do was go back in time to when she could still have childish fun.

When the game ended, Solana didn't even know who won until Jacie screamed, "We're going to the finals, Solana!"

Solana tried to sound cheery. "Would Stony Brook settle for anything less?"

"Becca's gonna want to celebrate," Tyler said, smacking his hands together and rubbing them with glee.

"She deserves it!" Nate said. "Let's take her to Crazy Charlie's for ice cream."

"I can't go," Solana said. "I have a test to study for."

Jacie put her hand on Solana's shoulder and looked at her with concern. "Are you okay? You're not acting like yourself."

Solana shrugged. "I'm just in a quiet mood tonight."

Jacie laughed. "I didn't know you had quiet moods. You sure you don't want to go with us? We won't be out late."

Solana looked at Jacie, wondering if she should go after all. This could be her chance to admit how she'd been feeling the last few days. She lowered her eyes and looked at the ground. *No*. In the eyes of her friends, she and Ramón had done something very wrong. Hearing a guilt-trip speech would feel worse than keeping quiet.

"I think I really need to get home."

The next day at school, Solana avoided her friends. During mid-morning break she went to the bathroom instead of the soda machine and touched up her heavy lipstick and eyeliner, something she hadn't worn in months. The *chola* look felt like a protective mask. Kids would look at the makeup, not at her.

At lunch she went to the library and buried her face in a book, hoping no one would see her. After lunch she sneaked into the back of English class to avoid Hannah and Becca. She pretended to listen to the teacher, when in reality, she could only think about Ramón. She missed him. She wanted to kiss him. She wanted to snuggle against his chest. But she didn't want the inevitable trip to the bedroom. The thought made her dread the evening ahead. It wasn't that she didn't like sex. She *did*. But her heart—the inside of her—was so mixed up about it. The puzzle pieces didn't fit right. Something was terribly wrong, and she couldn't figure out what it was.

How can I dread a Friday night with the boy who does nothing but make me feel special and loved?

When class ended, Solana tried to slip out quickly, but Becca met her at the door. "Solana, what's going on?"

"Nothing. I'm fine," Solana said. She ran her fingers through her hair, trying to look casual.

"Then what's with the *chola* look? You haven't done that since the beginning of school." Becca shifted her backpack. Her eyes and voice softened. "Did something happen with Ramón? Did you break up or something?"

The sweetness in Becca's voice brought tears to Solana's eyes. She fought to keep her voice steady. "No, we didn't break up."

"Something's wrong, though. Please talk to me, Solana. I know I was a huge brat over spring break and I'm really sorry. Whatever's wrong, you can tell your friends."

Solana blinked hard.

Becca touched her arm. "We can go somewhere after school and talk," Becca said.

Without stopping to think, Solana nodded. Even if her friends spouted off a sermon, she couldn't hold her confusion inside anymore. "Okay," she whispered.

"You want me to get Jacie and Tyler to come too, or should you and me talk by ourselves?"

"Jacie and Tyler," Solana said, feeling a desperate need to have all the support she could get. She looked around to make sure Hannah had gone on to her next class. "But not Hannah, okay?"

Becca nodded. "Where do you want to meet?"

Solana could think of only one place where she could pour out her heart freely to her friends and know that everything she said would be kept between them. She looked Becca in the eyes. "Alyeria."

chapter 18

Solana rode her bike to the playground of the elementary school where she, Becca, Tyler, and Jacie had become friends. The wind had picked up, and she pedaled hard against it. Patches of snow lay in shady spots on the ground. The closer she got to the school, the more slowly she rode, thinking over what to say once inside Alyeria.

When she reached the parking lot, she saw Tyler's and Jacie's cars. Solana rode her bike through the deserted playground. The swings squeaked in the wind, making it seem even more desolate. At the familiar cluster of aspen trees, Solana took a deep breath and told herself to relax. On the other side of those trees lay a safe place that only she and her friends shared.

When she poked through the bushes, she saw Tyler, Becca, and Jacie talking quietly. Becca moved to give Solana a hug. Solana hugged her back, not wanting to let go. When she did let go, she sat down on a log bench and let out a long sigh. Her friends gathered around, Becca sitting on one side and Jacie on the other. Tyler sat cross-legged on the ground.

"What's going on, Solana?" Jacie asked.

Tyler pushed his hair out of his eyes. "You've looked so sad ever since spring break."

Solana fought the tears welling up inside. Jacie whispered, "It's okay, Solana."

"It's just us," Becca said, stroking Solana's back.

Then the floodgates opened, and the tears wouldn't stop flowing, even as Solana spoke. "You know how I told you that Ramón and I started having sex?"

Everyone nodded.

"I told you it was so great."

"Wasn't it?" Jacie asked. She blushed and put her hand over her face for a second. "I mean, did something bad happen?"

"It was the perfect situation. He was sweet, gentle, romantic." Solana felt her cheeks grow red. "I'm so confused. The physical part was okay. Pilar says that it will get better and that I'll get over it. But I feel so awful inside. I don't understand. Ramón loves me and I love him. She's right. The more we do it the better things are physically, but I feel worse in my heart. It's empty—like I've lost a part of myself. And things between us feel so different now."

Solana looked at the frozen ground. "I tried to talk to my sister about it, but she told me I'd get over it. Well, I haven't gotten over it. Instead, it feels like the hole is growing."

Solana wiped her cheeks and waited for the sermon to start. Instead, she felt Becca's arms wrap around her. From the sound of Becca's breathing, Solana knew she was fighting back tears.

"Why didn't you tell us?" Becca's voice sounded tight.

"I'm so sorry you hurt," Jacie said, her voice breaking too.

Solana rested her head against Becca as her tears kept coming. "I didn't want to tell you guys," she sobbed. "I knew what you'd say—

that sex outside of marriage is wrong, that I shouldn't have done it, that you warned me. I just couldn't handle it."

Becca sniffled.

Tyler looked at her. "I can understand why you'd feel that way. But we're your friends, Solana. You can tell us anything."

Solana sat up and wiped her eyes with the sleeve of her jacket. She sniffed hard, glad to have Becca's arm still around her. Becca brushed tears from her own eyes. Solana looked away. *Why is Becca crying?*

Tyler put his hand on Solana's knee. "We all mess up. I think that's when we need our friends the most."

Solana nodded. "Thanks," she said, her voice barely a whisper.

"What next?" Jacie asked.

"Ramón and I are going to a movie tonight. The sad thing is, I know exactly how the date will end."

"It doesn't have to end with sex," Jacie said.

Becca squeezed her shoulder. "Just tell Ramón you don't want to do it anymore."

"I wish it were that easy. I've come close to saying that. But when I'm with him it's like, we can't go backward." She felt her cheeks grow red again. "In some ways I don't want to go backward. I keep thinking that this time will be different. This time it will be good both physically *and* emotionally."

"Should you break up?" Becca asked.

"I've never cared for a guy the way I care for Ramón. I've never had anyone treat me the way he does." Solana's tears returned. "I don't want to lose him."

"Ramón's a great guy," Jacie said. "So if he really cares about you, he'll listen and understand."

"And if he breaks up with you over sex, then he's not worthy of you anyway," Becca added.

"Whatever happens, the sex part has to stop," Tyler said, looking a little uneasy.

Solana hung her head. "I wish I'd waited. I don't like the confusion. And it feels like this hurt will never go away."

Jacie shifted around and sat cross-legged on the log bench, facing Solana. "Before you can sort things out, I think that you have to stop what's making you hurt in the first place."

"I know it'll be really hard," Becca said. "Just remember that no matter what happens, we'll be here for you. Jacie, Tyler, and I can pray that God helps you stop hurting so much."

Here we go, Solana thought. *Now they're going to lecture me about what God thinks.*

Jacie looked down at her hands. "Maybe we can pray now," she said hesitantly.

Solana wanted to say, "No, you guys do it on your own." Praying out loud for her seemed too weird.

"Is that okay, Solana?" Tyler asked.

She shrugged. Looking at her friends and seeing how much they cared made her say, "I guess."

Her friends closed their eyes, lowered their heads, and held hands, including her in the circle. She lowered her head but didn't close her eyes. As Becca started to pray, Solana looked at her shoes. They needed cleaning. She started to fidget. She crossed her legs and uncrossed them. Jacie gave her hand a gentle squeeze, and Solana began to relax. She began to listen to what her friends said as they took turns praying for her. Their prayers weren't like those she'd heard in church as a little girl. They didn't sound memorized or dull. Jacie, Becca, and Tyler were obviously talking to *someone.* Someone they respected and trusted—even thought of as a friend.

"Please give Solana the right words to say to Ramón," Jacie prayed. "And help him to be understanding, God."

Could God do that? Would He?

Tyler prayed for God to give her strength to stop the sexual part of her relationship. "Help her to know we love her no matter what happens."

Becca added, "And God, forgive me for acting in ways that made Solana feel she couldn't talk to me when she was hurting." She paused and took a deep breath. "God, I pray that You'll make Christ's love real to her. Help her to see how much she needs You, how much You care, that You gave Your life for her and are waiting to heal all her hurt and confusion. We pray all these things in Jesus' name, amen."

Solana kept her head down. How had the prayer managed to relax her so much? She felt at peace, as if everything might be okay no matter what happened with Ramón. Looking up, Solana noticed the looks on her friends' faces. She'd expected to get slammed. Instead, they surrounded her with love.

"Thanks," Solana said quietly.

Jacie gave her hand one more squeeze before letting go. "Anytime."

Solana looked at Becca. "I *really* am sorry about not going on the hike and for ignoring you all during spring break. That was pretty rude."

"Oh, I forgive you," Becca said.

"Thanks. I don't deserve it."

"Forgiveness is rarely deserved."

Solana lowered her eyes.

"Will you be okay?" Jacie asked. "What are you going to do?"

"I don't know," Solana said in a whisper. "It's so hard."

"Whatever you decide will be hard," Jacie said.

"But we'll be here for you," Becca said.

"Always," Tyler said, giving her hand a quick squeeze.

● ● ●

A few hours later, Solana walked out of the theater with Ramón. "How did you like the movie?" he asked.

Solana looked up at the star-filled sky, remembering the night at the observatory. *Why couldn't we have more nights like that?* "It was pretty good."

"The ending was kind of lame."

Solana nodded. She hadn't paid much attention to the movie. She slid into the car, growing tense with the knowledge of what she needed to say. She'd decided on her bike ride home from Alyeria—breaking up with Ramón was the right thing. At least it would be easier than risking his getting mad and breaking up with her.

Ramón hopped into the car and leaned over to kiss Solana's cheek. "You're quiet tonight."

"We were just at a movie."

"Yeah, but you were quiet before that, and you're even quieter now. Is anything wrong?"

She turned to face Ramón. "No," she said quietly.

"So, what do you want to do now?" He kissed Solana again. "Mom's working. You want to go to the apartment?"

How do I say this? If I let him take me to his mom's apartment, there'll be no turning back. I'll give in for sure. I just need to say it.

With her heart pounding, Solana pulled back from Ramón's kisses and said, "We'd better not."

She thought she'd cried all her tears at Alyeria. But here they were, stinging her eyes. A part of her wanted to go to the apartment and show Ramón that she still loved him. Everything in her felt connected to him, like he was literally a part of her and she a part of him.

"What is it?" Ramón put his fingers under Solana's chin and lifted her face.

"I don't know." When a tear rolled down her cheek, Ramón brushed it away with his thumb and pulled Solana close to him. With his arms around her, she felt so safe and protected—so loved. If they broke up, she'd never feel those arms around her again. *And how can I break up with someone I'm still in love with?*

"Talk to me, please."

Solana tried to pull away, but Ramón kept one arm around her, keeping her snuggled against his shoulder. "Ramón, I love you, but I don't want to go back to your apartment tonight. I mean I want to, but I can't. I can't . . . do that anymore." *I can't even say "sex." What is it that I can't do anymore? I want to be with him. I just don't want to end up in his bed again. Maybe he'll accept that. Maybe it's worth a try.*

Ramón turned to her and held her by the shoulders. "Have I done something to hurt you? If I have, I want to know. I never want to hurt you, Solana."

"Not what you've done, but what we've—oh, Ramón. I'm so confused. More than anything, I want to be with you, but every time we have sex, I go home feeling sad and empty. Then I feel horrible for feeling bad because you do nothing but treat me nice and make me feel good. I want to be with you, but I can't handle feeling like this anymore."

Ramón looked at Solana. "Are you saying you want to break up?"

"No," Solana said, unable to go through with her plan. *I love him too much. I can't . . .* "I just want to slow down and go back to the way things were before our night at the gazebo. Maybe the only way to do that is to not see each other so much—you know, so it's not so hard."

She waited for him to say that she couldn't have it both ways. That she was asking way too much.

"I care about *you*, Solana. Sure, what we've started doing has been great, but that's not what I'm in this for. If you need to slow down, then that's fine with me. It'll be hard, though, believe me."

"It'll be hard for me, too."

Ramón gently pulled Solana around to face him. He kissed her softly. When he sat back again, Solana saw the hurt and sadness in his eyes. Her heart ached more than ever, knowing she'd caused that hurt look. She expected him to say something else. Instead, he put his key in the ignition and started the car.

"Maybe I should take you home."

"That's probably a good idea."

"And after tonight, I'll leave things up to you. I won't push it by calling every day or anything. I'll wait to hear from you."

"Thanks." Inside, Solana felt unsettled. She hadn't lost Ramón—not for now, at least—and that filled her with relief. But could they really make this work?

chapter 19

All week long, Solana's feet felt heavy. She walked around school in a fog, just going through the motions of each class. Her friends didn't try to make her talk. Instead, they gave her more hugs than usual.

Solana appreciated the space they gave her. She expected to feel relieved that she and Ramón had talked and that everything would be okay. But inside, she felt a sense of doom. Since their talk, they'd spoken on the phone, but every conversation felt awkward. She ached to see him. At the same time, she knew she couldn't risk it. By Friday she plodded into the house.

Solana went to her room and dumped her backpack on the floor. She flopped on her bed and stared at the mural on the wall. Looking at those mustangs led by the unicorn foal filled her with sadness. They were free. *Will I ever feel free again?*

And then she saw it—the manila envelope lying on her desk chair.

After she opened it, she cried again. She crawled into her bed with her journal and pen and began to write.

As if life wasn't depressing and disappointing enough—It came today—a manila envelope from the science fair. You'd think I would have searched the mail every day for this. But with all this mess, I totally forgot about it. And when I saw how fat the envelope was, I KNEW it meant that I'd won. Yeah, right. Technically, I did win—if fourth place is anything to shout about. I didn't win the telescope and lost the chance for the scholarship I wanted so badly. No, I won magazine subscriptions. Oh, and a certificate to hang on my wall, immortalizing the fact that I wasn't quite good enough for first, second, or third. I don't know why I'm so surprised or why I'm so devastated. I knew when I saw the other projects that mine could never measure up. Still, I really needed something good to happen. How stupid of me to think anything would.

It's just that I feel like I've lost so much in the last couple of weeks.

Solana sat staring at her journal, trying to figure out how to express what she felt.

She'd lost her goal of winning the science fair. She'd lost her dreams of a telescope and, maybe, a scholarship. She'd lost the tender, fun relationship she had with Ramón. And she'd lost her virginity.

You didn't lose your virginity. You gave it away. You know exactly where it went.

Solana dropped her head, closing her eyes and letting thoughts surface at will.

You can't get virginity back again—ever.

The fog in her head began to clear. She began to see that some things in life happen only once. Birth. Death. Graduation from high school. Giving away your virginity.

These are all big events you can't repeat. No one takes those lightly, so why does everyone take sex lightly? Or virginity?

Solana sighed, the truth welling up within her.

I gave away a piece of myself. Why doesn't anyone tell you that sex is far more than just something physical?

She shuddered.

What does Hannah say? That "virginity is a gift given only once—"

Solana covered her face with her hands

Why did I laugh at her—at all of them? Why did I act like it's no big deal? Giving away my virginity WAS a big deal.

Solana lay her journal down, unable to write another word.

● ● ●

I really need Ramón right now, Solana thought as she left the house. She pictured him putting his arms around her and kissing her, saying how much her loved her whether she won the science fair or not. *I'll go to the ranch. It will be a natural way for me to see Ramón.*

Yet his car wasn't there when she arrived. A heaviness hung around Solana's heart. Feeling a lump rise in her throat again, Solana parked her bike and headed for the stables. She said little to her uncle, and in silence got Shadow ready to ride.

It had been so long since she'd ridden alone that the quiet of nature and the gentle rhythm of Shadow's hooves took awhile to have their usual calming effect on her. They came to the open pasture where the *puros tesoros* grazed. Instead of seeing them, she saw Ramón.

When did I become so completely attached to him?

It frightened her to need someone so much, to feel like she couldn't enjoy life without him. She tried to enjoy being with her friends the way she always had. But it wasn't working. Each day that passed, she felt more and more like a part of her was missing—as if someone had carved out a piece of her and walked away with it.

I have to stop needing Ramón so much.

She dismounted Shadow and stood watching the wild horses. She envied them. They would never know the sadness and confusion that consumed her.

Then she heard the footsteps of a shod horse on the trail. Turning, she expected to see a stranger. Instead she saw Ramón on Carmen, cantering toward her.

Solana stood still. She didn't wave. But her heart leapt within her.

"Whoa!" Ramón commanded Carmen. He dismounted and tied her to a tree.

Solana clutched Shadow's reins. She pictured her feet with roots holding her to the ground so she wouldn't run up to Ramón and throw herself into his arms like she yearned to do.

"Your uncle said you looked upset and rode off alone—I got a little worried."

"I told you before, I ride alone all the time." It felt easier to be annoyed with Ramón than to admit how much she needed him. "I know these trails like my own backyard."

"I know you do." Ramón walked closer. He reached his hand toward Solana's face, but then pulled back. "I just wanted to make sure you were okay."

I'll tell him about the science fair but nothing else. No, if I even tell him that, everything else will pour out, I'll cry, then he'll comfort me and kiss me, and we won't be able to stop.

Solana turned toward Shadow and stroked his mane. "I needed to think. And I like to ride alone when I'm thinking."

Ramón stroked Solana's hair. His touch made it so much more difficult to hold back. He leaned down and kissed her cheek. "I can help you think."

Warmth filled Solana's body. It had only been a week since she felt the warmth of Ramón's touch, but it seemed like so much longer. Without stopping to think, she turned to face him, and he kissed her. As they stood kissing, all her problems seemed to melt away. Ramón pulled back and pressed her head gently against his chest. She closed her eyes and enjoyed just being held by him, until he whispered, "Or we can go somewhere and help you forget what's bugging you."

Suddenly, all the emotions Solana had been fighting that day began to boil. Instead of tears, she burst in anger. "What are you talking about?" she spat as she pushed Ramón's arms away and stepped back. "You promised not to pressure me."

"I'm not trying to pressure you." Ramón seemed to stumble over his words. "I'm sorry, I just . . . I miss you. That just slipped out. It's been a week since I've seen you. I miss . . . being with you."

"*Being* with me how?" Solana didn't even wait for an answer. "You said you weren't with me for the sex, that you cared about *me*, but that's not really how you feel, is it?"

"I didn't say that." Ramón ran a hand through his hair, taking in long, frustrated breaths. "This is really hard, Solana. It's hard to hold back after being completely free with you."

It's hard for me, too. One minute I want to jump into your arms and the next, I don't want you touching me.

"Well," Solana said, "I don't understand why, if you say you care for and love me so much, you can't keep your hormones under control and back off like you promised." *What's my problem? Why am I being so mean to him?*

"I was just kissing you."

"But you want more."

Ramón hesitated before saying slowly, "Yes. I do want more."

Tears filled Solana's eyes, and she felt her lips trembling. "Even though you said we could slow down."

"Yes, I guess."

"Well, you can forget it."

She saw the hurt and confusion in Ramón's eyes and wanted to take every word back, but she couldn't.

"I'm not some kind of pervert."

"I know," Solana said, softening.

"Well, you're making me feel like one."

Solana looked at Shadow's feet. She leaned against his neck and sighed. She didn't think of him as a pervert, but she also didn't understand why he couldn't back off.

"Solana." Ramón stared off into the pasture where the *puros tesoros* grazed. "Maybe we did take things too fast. Maybe we *both* need some space and time to think."

"Yes." As much as her heart ached, she kept her emotions under control. Without another word, Ramón untied Carmen and rode back toward the ranch.

Once Ramón was out of sight, Solana's whole body shook with sobs. She pressed her face into Shadow's mane and wept harder than she could ever remember crying in her life. *I've lost Ramón*. How could loving one person be so excruciating?

When her tears subsided, she looked around her. Her sobs must have spooked the mustangs because they were gone. She couldn't go back to the ranch and face Ramón again. She couldn't stay on the mountain all night. What other option did she have? *I'll ride slow. Maybe Ramón will be gone by the time I get back.* Tugging on Shadow's reins, she mounted him and settled into the saddle. She nudged him with her heels.

I didn't have the chance to tell Ramón about my science project and what a loser I am.

She let Shadow go at his own pace. As he plodded along, every special moment that she and Ramón had shared together played in her mind. *We'll never have times like that again*. The thought brought a fresh flood of tears. Somewhere in her mind she should have known it would eventually come to this. Throughout her life, many adults had told her she couldn't have everything. How right they were! She couldn't have Ramón and expect him to give up the physical relationship they'd started. She couldn't have sex and think it wouldn't change their relationship in profound ways.

What will Becca, Jacie, and Tyler think? In the past, when she'd finished with a guy, she'd gone back to her friends and enjoyed them for a while before the next cute one walked by. This time felt different. Going back to everyday life and hanging out with her friends like nothing had changed wasn't possible. Going out with other guys seemed even less possible. *Hannah will be pleased.* But, she had to admit to herself, Hannah had been nothing but compassionate. *Even though Hannah will be glad, she won't show it.*

Solana found a large rock, dismounted Shadow, and sat, her thoughts drifting back to the day at Alyeria. Her friends were supportive, even though she'd made a choice they considered immoral. They didn't lecture her like she expected, and they didn't minimize her feelings like Pilar did. They simply listened and cried with her.

They even prayed for me, knowing I'd probably give them a hard time about it. They prayed for my relationship, even though, in their eyes, I messed up with Ramón.

"We don't want to see you get your heart broken," Jacie had said. Solana remembered how sure of herself she felt when she insisted that Ramón would never break her heart.

"Ramón may not, but the consequences of your decision might." The memory of Hannah's words stung. How could she have been so right? The girl who knew nothing about dating. How could she know such a thing?

But everything seemed so perfect. Everything was *perfect. He loves me and I love him. He didn't just care about getting me into bed; he cared about* me. *I thought sex brought people closer.*

She thought about that a moment. It *did* bring her and Ramón closer—*but it is also tearing us apart. How is that possible?*

Solana got up, unable to sit alone with her thoughts anymore. She got back on Shadow and they continued down the trail. The closer she got to her uncle's ranch, the more she dreaded actually reaching it and seeing Ramón. How would she handle going to the ranch now? Maybe she'd stay away for a while. No, the ranch was one of her favorite places to spend time. She'd just have to learn to deal with it. What would be harder, she wondered, dealing with seeing or learning to live without Ramón?

• • •

Mama's voice woke Solana out of a fitful night's sleep. Her head felt glued to the pillow as she fought to open her eyes.

"*Mi'ja*," Mama said, putting her hand to Solana's forehead. "It's past ten. Are you feeling okay?"

"Yeah." Solana's voice was hoarse. "I just didn't sleep well."

Mama held the phone out to her. Solana saw the worry on her face and made up her mind to start acting normal before Mama started asking questions.

"It's Becca."

Solana sat up and blinked hard against the sunlight pouring through her window. "Hello." Her mother left and shut the door.

"Hi," Becca said. "Are you okay? You weren't at the game last night."

"What game?"

"The final *championship* game," Becca said. Solana closed her eyes tight and punched her pillow. She waited for Becca to get mad. Instead, Becca stayed quiet.

"Becca, I'm sorry. I totally forgot." She couldn't remember even hearing about it. The last week had been such a blur. Solana rested against her headboard. "I was really upset last night." She swallowed hard, feeling a return of the deep sadness from the day before. "Ramón and I broke up yesterday."

"Solana, I'm sorry."

"I guess I knew it was coming."

"Yeah, but it still hurts."

"Yeah, a lot." It hurt too much to talk about Ramón, so she changed the subject. "So, how was the game?"

"We won. But that's not what's important right now."

"Of course it is. I knew you'd take Stony Brook to victory."

Becca was quiet for a moment, then asked, "Are you sure you're okay?"

Solana took in a deep breath and let it out slowly. "You know me. I'll be fine."

"What are you doing today?"

"Nothing. Sitting at home picking out magazine subscriptions, I guess."

"Magazine subscriptions?" Becca asked.

"Another major blow. As if losing my boyfriend wasn't enough. I got fourth in the district science fair. For my big prize, I get three thrilling magazine subscriptions."

"Fourth place is good, Solana," Becca said earnestly. "But I know you wanted to place higher than that."

"And magazine subscriptions? What an insult!"

"Yeah, especially when you wanted the telescope. It's hardly the same thing."

Solana sat up. "Maybe I can pick out a magazine about telescopes."

"Or one that has a big poster of a telescope inside."

"Hey, yeah! See, I feel better already."

"Really, Solana," Becca said, "call me if you want to talk, okay?"

"I will."

"Promise?"

"I promise. And this time I mean it."

After Becca hung up, Solana got out of bed. She showered and ate breakfast. Then she volunteered to clean the kitchen so Mama could get started on her errands. Solana wanted the house to herself so she could think undisturbed.

As soon as Mama walked out the door, Solana began to scrub everything in sight. Her thoughts zeroed in on Ramón. Her heart tightened as though someone squeezed it and wouldn't let go. She vigorously scrubbed the counter by the stove with her sponge, trying to chase away that feeling. They'd had so many good times. Why couldn't she think about *them* instead?

So she did. Yet she found that dwelling on those memories hurt even more.

Solana looked around the kitchen, saw nothing else to clean, and decided to vacuum the living room. When she finished cleaning, she thought, *Maybe I'll rearrange my room.*

A loud knock at the door almost made her jump out of her skin.

chapter 20

Solana heard familiar voices outside. She felt her heart sink. *I guess I was hoping it was Ramón.*

When Solana opened the door, Becca announced, "We're kidnapping you." She, Jacie, Hannah, and Tyler all stood on the front porch, dressed in warm clothes and hiking shoes.

"Put on your hiking shoes and get a coat, a bottle of water, and some money," Jacie ordered. "You have three minutes, young lady." She giggled. "Okay, five."

Looking at her friends, Solana stood there with her mouth open. "Okay," she said finally.

"So," Tyler said. "Are you going to make us wait out here in the cold, or do we get to come in?"

Solana stepped aside. "What's going on?" she asked, following them into the living room.

"Becca called and said you need to do something fun," Hannah explained.

"I actually have a whole Saturday off," Jacie said, flopping down on the couch. "That almost never happens."

"So, go!" Tyler smacked Solana on the shoulder and pointed to the stairs. "Get your stuff."

"Consider this a second chance to take that hike at the falls." Becca flopped down beside Jacie.

Solana looked at each of her friends, not knowing what to say. Their timing was so perfect it was almost eerie.

"Go!" they all said together.

Solana smiled and ran to get her hiking boots from her closet. In the kitchen, she grabbed a water bottle that would fit in the pocket of her jacket. When she got back to the living room, the group was talking to Papa, who'd come in from the backyard. Becca was explaining the kidnapping plot to him.

"You kids are good friends," Solana's father said to Becca. "Solana won't tell us why she's been moping around the house so much, but whatever it is, getting some fresh air and being with friends will be good for her."

Solana waited out of sight, listening to the concern in Papa's voice. She hadn't told her parents that she broke up with Ramón for fear they'd ask why. *I'd better tell them soon.*

"Ready," Solana said to her friends. She gave her father a hug. "See you later, Papa."

Papa pulled her into a tight hug and kissed her on both cheeks. "Have a fun day, *mi'ja.*"

"I will."

"Bye, Mr. Luz," they all said on the way out.

Outside, they piled into Jacie's car. "Let Solana ride shotgun," Jacie said. "This is her day."

Solana settled in her seat. *What if Ramón calls?* Solana blinked hard, afraid that just thinking about him might start her crying again.

As good as it felt to be surrounded by her friends, a part of her wanted to be with Ramón. She felt like she belonged in a different world. Her friends talked about last night's championship game, which only made Solana feel more disconnected.

"Solana, it was the best game," Jacie said. "When I got there after work, it was tied. Then Katie went one-on-one with that Ashley girl again and made the winning basket, right as the buzzer went off."

"Man, I don't know what's happened to Katie, but I hope it lasts," Becca said. "Even if she *is* starting to make me look like a klutz."

"She is not," Tyler insisted. "You scored twenty points to her six."

"I have pictures to prove it," Hannah told her.

"Sorry I missed it," Solana said, unable to think of anything else to say.

At the trailhead, everyone piled out of the car and grabbed their gear. Solana followed the others automatically, without thought or emotion. As they moved up the trail chattering back and forth, Solana could only hear the soothing rush of Misty Falls in the distance. The sound triggered memories of kissing Ramón after their date to the Copper Mining Company. She didn't realize that she'd slowed down until Jacie called to her, "Come on, Solana. We're losing you, girl."

She watched her friends bounding up the trail. They looked so happy and worry-free. Did they understand her hurt at all? Becca, Jacie, and Tyler had all dated. But they often talked about trying to put their relationship with God ahead of romantic relationships. It wasn't easy, but it was their goal. *Could God really take the place of someone who can kiss and touch and hold you?*

Then there was Hannah. Solana watched the tall blonde, who could probably have her pick of any guy in the school. Her plan to court, not date, seemed so old-fashioned, so confining. Yet Hannah seemed so happy with her family's rules on courtship that she'd even made them her own. Like the others, Hannah was more concerned about her relationship with God than anything else. *Do my friends actually love God more than guys?*

Solana was so lost in her thoughts that she didn't even notice how far they'd walked. Suddenly, she became aware that they were stopping at the top of one of the cliffs overlooking the falls.

Becca dropped her backpack. "Mom packed lunches for us," she announced as she handed out sack lunches to everyone.

"Your mom is the best," Tyler said.

"I'll pray for all of us," Becca said after everyone had their sack. "God, thank You for this beautiful day and for this food. Thanks for letting Solana be with us again, and I pray this day cheers her up. In Jesus' name, amen."

As the prayer ended, Solana realized that she'd closed her eyes and bowed her head along with her friends. Before her friends could catch her and make a big deal about it, she opened her lunch, pulling out a wrapped bologna and cheese sandwich, a bag of chips, an apple, and a can of orange soda.

"Perfect picnic food," Tyler said, opening his soda. "Nothing with any nutritional value whatsoever—except the apple."

"There's a package of Girl Scout cookies in my backpack for later," Becca said with her mouth full of sandwich.

"Wow!" Tyler said, shoving the remainder of his sandwich into his mouth. "What kind? Not that it matters, because those Girl Scouts know how to do cookies."

Everyone laughed, and Solana smiled. *A real smile*, she thought, surprising herself.

Everyone managed to talk nonstop and eat at the same time. Solana just listened. When a ground squirrel scampered by, she tossed it some crust from her sandwich.

Jacie got up from her spot beside Hannah and joined Solana on the ground, bringing her lunch with her. "You're never as quiet as you've been lately, Sol. Are you okay?"

Solana nodded and took a sip of soda.

"You sure?" Becca asked. "Really, if you want to talk . . ."

Solana took a deep breath.

"You miss Ramón a lot, huh?" Jacie said.

Solana nodded.

"I know because when I had to break things off with Damien, I missed him all the time, even though I knew I was doing the right thing." A faraway look came to her eyes. "I thought about him all the time. It didn't help that I had that stupid painting to remind me of everything."

Pulling at the plastic wrap around her sandwich, Solana admitted, "I wish our last talk hadn't turned out the way it did."

"Maybe you'll get to talk again," Hannah said. "When you've both had some time."

"I hope so." Solana took a small bite of her sandwich and chewed slowly. She had a hard time swallowing. "How do you all do it?" she asked before she could stop herself. "When I started dating Ramón, I was the happiest I'd ever been. Even before that, I have always been happiest and felt the best about myself when I had a guy. How can you not need guys in your life?"

"Well," Tyler said, stretching back to relax. "I can't say I've ever needed guys to make me content. I'm completely fine without 'em."

Becca tossed a corn chip at him. "She's asking a serious question, Tyler."

"Oh, okay." Tyler looked at Solana and wiggled an eyebrow. "Sorry to ruin the moment."

"Well?" Solana looked at Jacie and Becca.

"You want my honest answer?" Jacie asked.

"Uh, *yeah*," Solana said. "Honesty would be good."

"Okay, I'd love to have a boyfriend. But you remember what happened with Damien. Because of him, I wasn't honest with you guys. All my thoughts focused on him and spending time with him. Worse, though, I started putting him before God. When that gets out of balance, everything starts to go haywire. God has to be first, or nothing else in life works right."

"But how can God take the place of a boyfriend? He's not a flesh-and-blood person." Ramón's soft kisses and tender touches swam through Solana's head, bringing back that sweet warmth she missed so much. "God can't hug you or kiss you or say nice things to you. Is it so wrong to want that stuff?"

"No," Becca said before Jacie could answer. "We all want that. And I think God made us to need those things. It's when we take physical stuff too far or too soon that it's wrong."

"It's hard for all of us," Hannah said. "Not just you. I mean, I know that God is supposed to fill all my needs, but there are times when I need a hug or some kind of human touch. Then I feel bad because God doesn't seem to be enough."

Solana eyed Hannah carefully. *She struggles with these things too?*

Jacie smiled at Hannah, then at Solana. "You know what's great, though? Since I've been getting closer to God, I've started admitting my feelings and needs for hugs and kisses to Him. When I do, He either takes away the aching need or sends something to help me at the right time. Someone will give me a hug exactly when I need one, or say something nice. The weirdest one is when I feel as if I've somehow been hugged. It's as if God Himself hugged me."

"Well, what about you, Becca?" Solana asked after a moment.

Becca shrugged. "What do you mean? I *have* a guy in my life."

"Well, don't you ever want to be alone with Nate more? You know, so you can kiss and snuggle without people seeing."

Becca blushed. "Yes. That's exactly why my parents want me to spend more time with groups. There are way too many temptations that come with dating one-on-one. Sometimes Nate looks at me a certain way and I'm like, good thing we're not alone because if we started to kiss, who knows where we'd end up."

Solana looked at Becca. "Are you saying that you might be tempted to fool around with him or have sex? *You?*"

Becca's cheeks turned an even deeper shade of red. "Well, yeah. I *am* human, Solana. Just because I'm a Christian doesn't mean I don't have the same thoughts and temptations that you do. But I made a commitment to stay pure until I get married. So I have to set limits and stick to them. If I didn't, I'd be in big trouble in no time. My parents have helped me with some of those personal rules. That's why I'm not allowed to have a boy in the house when my parents are gone. You know, stuff like that."

"Glad to hear I'm not the only one who has to set limits in advance," Tyler admitted. "It was always hard to be alone with Jessica. So many times I had to drill it into my own head that once Jessica and I took a step physically, we couldn't *untake* it."

Solana lowered her voice. "You got that right."

"Um." Hannah cleared her throat. "I don't know anything about what you're going through. But it's just been on my heart to say this, Solana. I know you're really hurting because of losing Ramón. At the same time, you've lost something that you can't get back. That must be really hard to deal with."

Everyone looked at Hannah. Solana remembered how she'd changed the subject at Sofa City Diner before Hannah could hear what she'd done with Ramón.

Hannah pushed back some loose hair. "I know you didn't want me to know, but it was pretty easy to figure out."

Appreciating that Hannah had kept quiet, Solana said, "It's okay if you know."

Hannah moved closer to Solana. "No matter what you've lost, Solana, your heart can be healed. You might not get Ramón back, and God can't give you your virginity back, but Christ can make you new inside."

Solana sighed loudly. *Just what I didn't want to hear, that Jesus is the answer to all my problems.*

"He can give you the forgiveness that you need and help you start all over again."

"Forgiveness?" Solana asked, irritability coming out in her voice. Needing healing from her hurt made sense, but *forgiveness?* "Look, I know you think what I did was a sin. But how can I be sinning if I don't choose to live under God's rules?"

"Because God's ways are truth whether you choose to follow them or not." Hannah's voice softened. "He created sex for marriage. If you do it outside that protective place, you hurt because you went against God's plan."

Solana shook her head. This wasn't where she wanted the conversation to go. She waited for someone to contradict Hannah, to say she had it all wrong. Nobody did. Looking around at her friends, a question came to mind that she was almost afraid to ask. "Do you guys look down on me now, as this big bad sinner?"

Jacie put her arm around Solana. "No way."

"No." Becca moved close to Jacie and Solana.

"You're our friend no matter what," Tyler said.

Hannah gave Solana a kind, reassuring smile. "We all do things that are sinful, whether we're Christian or not."

"We love you, Solana," Becca said. "It's just that, well, like in our promise in Alyeria, we want the best for you."

"The 'best' meaning having Christ in my life?"

Becca looked into Solana's eyes. "We'll always want that for you."

"We know how He's changed our lives and want the same thing for you," Hannah said. "Just think of it this way: Unlike guys, Jesus will always be there."

"Yeah. He'll never break up with you." Jacie smiled at Solana. Something about her sunshiny smile made Solana smile too.

Tyler snorted. "That's one way to put it, Jace."

Hannah pulled her knees up to her chest and smiled sweetly at Jacie. "I don't think I could have put it any better."

"And we're here for you no matter what," Becca said.

Solana nodded. "I know."

Taking a deep breath, Becca looked around. "So, does anyone want a cookie?"

"Maybe later." Solana stuffed her unfinished lunch into the paper bag.

"Speak for yourself." Tyler reached for Becca's pack. "Hand 'em over."

"In the car," Becca said, clutching the pack to her chest. "I don't want you eating them all before anyone else gets their fair share."

"Life isn't fair," Tyler said.

Becca glared at him.

"Okay, okay," Tyler said, putting up his hands in surrender.

Solana felt lighter inside, knowing her friends still accepted her, that they actually understood and had temptations themselves. But the last half of their talk didn't click. *I still don't get how Jesus can help anything. It doesn't make sense.*

Everyone stuffed their trash into Becca's backpack and started down the trail.

On the ride home, Jacie put in a cassette tape, and Becca broke out the cookies. Solana noticed her friends looking over at her once in a while, like they wanted to make sure she was okay.

"Thanks for the hike," she said when Jacie drove into Solana's driveway. "I really did have fun. I would have moped around the house all day otherwise. I mean, between Ramón and the science fair, I was pretty bummed out."

"We heard," Tyler said. He gripped Solana's shoulder. "So sorry, Sol."

"We thought it best not to bring it up," Jacie said. Hannah nodded, her eyes full of understanding.

"Thanks," Solana said, wishing she could say more. But emotions blocked the words.

"We'll always see you as a genius," Jacie told her. "So if you feel bad about yourself, hang out with us and we'll make you feel better. You're way smarter than we'll ever be."

chapter 21

Solana flopped onto her bed. Tears streamed down her cheeks. Did Ramón miss her as much as she missed him? The thought of never being able to make things right with him brought a flood of grief that she could no longer hold back. She stuffed her face into her pillow and sobbed.

After a few minutes, she sat up. *I need to calm down.* She wiped her eyes and went to her desk drawer to find her journal. Solana wanted to write about what was on her mind, but no words would come. She only stained the pages with a new flood of tears.

I'll call him, she decided. *He's probably waiting for me to make the next move. He probably thinks I don't care. Or that I don't love him anymore. But I do. Sorry, my friends, but an invisible God just can't take his place.*

She started planning a speech in her mind. She'd apologize, then tell him how much she cared for him and wanted him back, no matter what. Even if it meant continuing sex. If that's what it took to keep him, she'd do it.

Solana got up to get the phone. But something stopped her. How would she explain this to her friends after the long talks they'd had? *None of them have ever really been in love. And they've never had sex, either. They don't understand how I feel. Why do I feel I should have to explain anything? This is my choice—what I feel is best for me.*

But was it? She thought about her planned speech again and realized how pathetic it sounded. She sat on her bed and started to cry. Reality told her that to call Ramón when she felt desperate would be a bad idea.

By the time Solana ran out of tears, the sun was going down, and she could smell tamales cooking in the kitchen.

Mama knows tamales are my favorite. She's trying to cheer me up without even knowing what's wrong.

Not wanting her tear-stained face to be obvious, Solana took a shower and reapplied her makeup. Thankful she was too worn out to think about Ramón, or her friends, or God, or anything else, she went downstairs for dinner.

• • •

Solana couldn't sleep. The conversations and prayers with her friends played over and over in her mind.

My friends make everything sound so simple. At the same time, their words had her all hung up inside. It didn't surprise her that they brought up God. After all, that's what they always did. But why did Jesus always have to come into it—like He was the only way to God? That was so narrow-minded. And why had Hannah mentioned forgiveness? The others seemed to agree with her. But none of them looked down on Solana. How could that be?

When the sun came up, Solana wondered if she'd slept at all. She heard her parents downstairs getting ready for mass. She knew her friends were on their way to church as well. *Everyone I know is going somewhere to be with God today.*

She wondered if it were truly possible to connect with something bigger than herself. Was there someone who could give her some answers and help her find peace again?

She waited until her father's car pulled out of the driveway before going downstairs and pouring a bowl of cereal. She ate mechanically, numb from emotions and lack of sleep.

When Solana finished her breakfast, she returned to her room. She shoved her journal and a pen into her purse. "I'll go to where I last felt peace," she whispered to herself.

● ● ●

Solana pedaled her bike through the empty elementary school playground. The fact that she once was small enough to play on the pint-sized equipment and drink from the short drinking fountains seemed so bizarre. She could almost see the smaller version of herself—carefree, sassy attitude, always anxious to play and imagine. But never in her games did she imagine life as a "big girl" could be so full of pain and unanswered questions.

Once inside Alyeria she stood, soaking in the quiet beauty of it. Every detail of her previous visit came back to her. She saw the loving concern in the eyes of her friends. She felt their listening silence as she poured out her heart. But she didn't want to remember the sincere way they talked to God.

For a brief moment she envied her friends' faith that allowed them to be so content, so sure about who they were and what they believed. *Does faith in God really make such a big difference in someone's life?*

Yeah. It makes you act like a narrow-minded weirdo who can't see reality.

She put her head in her hands. *But my friends aren't like that, are they?*

Well, sometimes they are. They can be so judgmental.

Suddenly it struck her that *she*, Solana Mariana Luz, was really the judgmental one. They didn't judge her. They simply had standards they lived by and believed in. Was that so bad? They believed in truth that doesn't change, while she didn't. How could ultimate truth for all people be possible? There were so many ways of looking at life, relationships, and spiritual journeys. Did God expect everyone to be clones of each other? *I could never believe in a God who wanted everybody to be exactly alike.*

Solana slapped her thighs and got up and paced. "Does it really matter what I believe?" she said out loud to no one—or to God—she wasn't really sure.

"Do the specifics of what anyone believes really matter that much?"

Her parents seemed to draw a lot of comfort from their faith. Mama prayed and lit candles when people were sick or died, and this seemed to help her deal with whatever she was concerned about. Even Katie Spencer spoke of prayer. Her friends took it a step further, saying the most important thing was what a person believed about Christ.

That's where they lose me, Solana thought. *Isn't it enough just to believe in God and try to be more spiritual in whatever way works for you?*

The prayer of her friends returned to her. She recalled the peace that had filled Alyeria while her friends prayed. They had all seemed so at ease talking to God. A part of her wanted to feel like she could pour out her problems anytime and know someone real was listening. But did she really need to pray, or did she only feel that way now because of the hurt over Ramón? It seemed awfully weak to her that people always had to go running to God as if He were their Big Daddy. Couldn't they just be strong enough on their own?

Solana reached into her purse and pulled out her journal and pen. She plunked herself on the ground and leaned against the log. She pulled her knees up and started writing. She wrote fast, her thoughts pouring out on the pages.

Hannah says I disobeyed God's plan by sleeping with Ramón. That doesn't make any sense to me. How can I disobey someone that I don't choose to let rule my life? Don't God's rules only apply to those who want to follow the Bible? Frankly, if God is punishing me for disobeying one of His rules, that's entirely unfair. It would be like me disobeying Katie Spencer's curfew and then getting punished for it.

There's no way it was wrong to sleep with Ramón. We didn't just jump into bed with someone we hardly knew. We loved each other. We still do. We didn't just jump into sex one night without thinking about it. We planned it all out so it would be perfect, and it was!

She stopped writing. She tapped her pen on the side of the journal, staring off into the grove.

Well. If it wasn't wrong, then why do I still feel weird about it?

Solana stared at the words. She didn't want to contemplate what truth might lie hidden behind them. She wrote quickly again.

I miss Ramón. I miss the fun we had before everything changed. I wish I could go back in time. I wish I had answers.

She shook her head. Her friends didn't give her answers; they talked to God. Solana took a deep breath, afraid of what she was about to do next.

Write a prayer to God?

Not Solana Luz.

She shivered. "Well," she said aloud, "it's not really a prayer if it's written. And it's not really a prayer if I don't believe everything that goes with it, right?"

She bent her head over her journal and began to write, afraid the trees might see and tell on her.

Solana Luz is praying.

Sheesh! If her friends found out, she'd never live it down. But she wrote anyway.

> My friends say I need you, God. That You're the only one who can really heal the hurt I feel inside.
>
> God, I don't know if I want to believe in who my friends say You are. But I guess I want to keep a more open mind. Don't expect too much. I still have lots of questions. And they certainly aren't going to be answered in one day. And I'm not going to swallow everything I'm told—got it?

She slammed the journal shut and stuffed it back into her purse. She squeezed back through the bushes, wondering whether or not she should tell her friends that she was thinking about having a more open mind about God.

No, she decided. *Then they'll pressure me to go to church and youth group meetings. Hannah will buy me a Bible, and Becca will ask me every week if I've read it. I need to do this in my own way for now.*

One thing she knew for sure. No matter what her conclusion about God would be, she knew she couldn't look at her friends in the same light ever again. They'd proved her conclusions about them were wrong. And maybe she was wrong about other things as well.

She closed her eyes and sighed. *I can't deal with that right now.*

●●●

Solana went home to an empty house. Spying the phone, she picked it up and played with it.

Maybe it's time to call Ramón.

She put it down.

No.

She sat on the sofa. She stared at the phone.

He's probably not home.

Worse, he probably doesn't want to talk to me.

She leaned over and took the phone off the table. She took a deep breath and dialed Ramón's number.

The phone rang three times before Ramón picked up. "Hello."

"Hi, Ramón," Solana said, feeling that her voice sounded like a little girl's. "It's me, Solana."

His voice softened. "How are you?"

"Okay." She took the phone up the stairs to her room. "I wanted to say I'm sorry about the other day."

"Me, too."

"I've been really confused, since . . ."

Ramón cut her off. "I know. Me, too." He paused. "It's like that night changed everything."

"Can we ever really go back to the way things were before?"

Ramón took a deep breath. "I don't know. I was sure that I could, but then when I saw you on the trail, it seemed totally impossible. Maybe it's one of those things that people can't go backward with."

Solana felt tears welling up and couldn't keep them from spilling. "What are we supposed to do now?"

"I don't know."

"I don't want you to quit working at the ranch because of me. You love working there, and Manuel really likes you."

"I thought about that. I almost gave notice the other day because I couldn't handle this. But you're right. I can't quit. And I don't want you to stay away from the ranch because of me."

This is going to be so hard no matter what we do.

"I won't." Secretly she knew that for a while she wouldn't go to the ranch as often. It would be too hard.

"Maybe if we see each other at the ranch, we can relearn how to be friends. You know, start over."

Solana wondered, *can we really?* "Yeah, maybe."

"Solana," Ramón said. "I'm glad you called. I wanted to call you, but I'd made up my mind that you had to make the next move. So, thanks."

"I'm glad I did too." She didn't want to think about what might have happened if she hadn't. Things would have been left the way they were on the trail the other day.

For a few minutes she and Ramón tried to talk about everyday things, like the horses and school. Solana told Ramón about getting fourth place in the science fair. "I'm sorry," he said. "I know how much you wanted first."

Tears rolled down her cheeks. She kept quiet so he wouldn't know she was crying again. The silence stretched. But Solana couldn't speak. She didn't know what to say.

"I still love you, Solana."

"I love you too."

Solana felt lighter when she hung up with Ramón. They still loved each other. Maybe that needed to be enough for now.

chapter 22

By Monday, Solana was tired from such an emotional weekend but somehow stronger at the same time. At least everything wasn't bound up inside her anymore. For the first time since spring break, she felt her old self returning, even though a part of her still seemed to be missing. Each guy with dark, curly hair she passed in the halls made her think of Ramón, and the hurt in her heart returned. She kept telling herself, *At least I have mostly good memories. And he still cares about me. Maybe we'll eventually be able to get back together.*

At lunch she searched out her friends in the cafeteria. She made up her mind as she approached the lunch table. *Today, I want to be myself.*

"Solana," Becca said, patting the place next to her. "Come sit."

Solana sat down and pulled her lunch out of her backpack. Looking around the table, she could tell she'd shown up in the middle of a conversation. Jacie was passing around a flyer while Hannah said something about not wanting to listen to certain types of music, even if it *did* fall under the category of Christian.

"We got a deejay who promises to play all kinds of Christian music. He promised to play mostly the ones we all listen to." Jacie rattled off a list of Christian bands, some that Solana didn't recognize, and a couple others that she'd heard riding in her friends' cars.

"I'm sure the evening will be okay with your parents," Becca said.

"But an all-night event with boys?" Hannah said, shaking her head.

"It's sponsored by The Edge. It will be very well chaperoned," Jacie said. "They've never had a problem yet."

Solana leaned forward to rest her arms on the table and looked at Hannah. "Would this group ever lead you down the road to ruin? I don't think so. Tell your parents you *really* want to go. The event is *Christian*. Hello! How bad can it be?"

Jacie grinned at Solana. "It looks like the old Solana's back."

Solana took a bottle of lime-flavored mineral water out of her bag and plunked it on the table. "Looks like it."

Hannah studied the flyer. "If they can call one of the leaders to check it out, maybe they'll let me. How much are the tickets?"

"Fifteen," Jacie said. "Which is a great deal for eight hours at Crazy Charlie's Fun Center. We can do anything there—the go-carts, miniature golf, arcade—"

"Batting cages," Becca added.

Tyler set down his half-eaten sandwich. "Maybe they'll have an open mike session for us on their little stage. I can bring my guitar and have my big debut."

Becca covered a smile. "Uh, I'm pretty sure they won't."

As her friends talked about the all-night event—how they'd get there, who to invite, who would win on the go-cart race track—Solana tried to eat her lunch. Usually, she avoided their Christian activities. She'd been to Christian summer camp a couple times. But she always stayed away from Bible studies and Christian conventions. She took a bite of her leftover tamale and listened to her friends' excitement.

Maybe the all-nighter would be fun—if it wasn't filled with a bunch of God-talk.

Just when Solana was ready to ask Jacie more about the event, Katie Spencer walked by, balancing a personal-sized pizza on top of her biology book.

"Hey, Katie!" Becca called to her. She grabbed one of the flyers from Jacie's stack.

"The Edge is going to sponsor an all-night event at Crazy Charlie's next weekend." Becca held the flyer out to her. "Want to go?"

Katie took the flyer and looked at it before handing it back to Becca. "It sounds fun, but I have my own overnighter planned that weekend. Sorry."

"Well, maybe the next one."

"Yeah, maybe." Katie smiled before turning to leave.

"So." Solana reached for the flyer in Becca's hand. "Do I get one of those? I mean, if you offered one to Katie."

"Sure," Becca said. She let Solana take the flyer.

Solana casually read it, feeling four sets of eyes studying her. The flyer listed all that would be available to them. She noted there wasn't any small print mentioning a speaker.

"Would you be interested in going?" Hannah asked, narrowing her eyes.

Solana shrugged. "I might."

"As long as I've been part of this group, you've never wanted to attend any events The Edge has sponsored."

"Yeah, well, this one sounds fun. Crazy Charlie's isn't too bad." She smiled mischievously, then looked at her friends. "Is it *okay* if I go, or is this a Christians-only thing?"

"Of course you can go," Becca said, sitting on the edge of her seat. "I was going to invite you, only Katie walked by before I had a chance." She looked across the table at Hannah. "We always invite Solana, even when she keeps saying 'no.' "

"And see," Tyler added, "sometimes she surprises us."

"I promise to be a good girl, okay?" Solana blinked her eyes angelically.

Tyler punched Solana in the arm. "We'll keep you in line."

Solana punched Tyler back.

Jacie grinned and stuffed the remaining flyers into her backpack. "It'll be the whole group of us, then. This is going to be so fun!"

"Yeah," Becca said. She and Solana locked eyes, exchanging a look of understanding. "It's nice to have you back, Solana."

"Even if you are back to your old, brutal self." Tyler rubbed his arm and grimaced like Solana had really hurt him.

"And you look like you're doing better," Jacie said to Solana. "Are you?"

"Yes, I am."

"Have you talked to Ramón yet?" Jacie shook her head in frustration. "I'm sorry. I promised myself I wouldn't ask, but—well, you know my mouth. It sometimes talks without asking permission."

"That's okay." Suddenly, sitting among her friends, talking about Ramón didn't feel so heartbreaking. "We talked yesterday. A lot of things are better now. I mean, we didn't get back together, but we're not mad at each other anymore."

"Good," Jacie said.

"We both admitted we moved too fast and now we need to start over. If that's even remotely possible—and I have huge doubts that it is. For now, we're going to try giving each other some space."

She looked around the table at her group of faithful friends. "Thanks for everything, you guys. You've really been there for me lately, even though I did something you don't think is right. I mean, you could have said, 'Forget you,' and let me go through the hard parts by myself."

"We're there for each other no matter what. You know that," Jacie said.

"Even if you are wild and boy-crazy and out of control," Tyler said.

Becca wrapped one arm around Solana and playfully pulled her close. "Oh, how could we ever turn our backs on you? You're our Sis. Our . . ."

Solana held up one hand to cut her off. "Don't *even* say the *Brio* Sis thing. I mean, aren't we getting a little old for stuff like that?"

"Never!"

"That's right." Tyler smacked the table. "We're never too old for the *Brio* Sis thing!"

Jacie looked at him and laughed. "But *some* of us might be too masculine, Bro."

Everyone cracked up. Solana sat up straight. She grabbed one of Tyler's tortilla chips, held it out to him, then stuck it in her own mouth.

Hannah tucked her long hair back behind her ear. "I really hope you'll go to the all-nighter with us, Solana. I hope you'll tag along with us more, wherever we go."

"Well, don't push it." Solana reached for another one of Tyler's chips, but he smacked her hand away. She flicked a crumb of her tamale toward him and went back to eating her own lunch. She smiled to herself. It felt good to do immature things with her friends again.

"Solana." Dennis Sanchez took a seat on the bench beside her. "Did you hear anything about the science fair yet?"

Solana glanced around the table at her friends, who sent her sympathetic looks. She covered her face and groaned, then turned to smile at Dennis. "How would *you* like a free magazine subscription of your very own? I have three, and you can have one of them."

Dennis squinted at Solana. "I don't get it. What's that have to do with the science fair?"

Solana laughed again. "I'll tell you later." She patted the table. "Join us. It's been awhile since we hung out."

"Can't," Dennis said. "I have a date with the library. My chemistry homework looms like a giant female mantis, ready to devour me at any moment."

As Dennis walked away, Solana noticed Cameron at a nearby table. *I wonder what would have happened if he hadn't been such a jerk and things had worked out with us? He wouldn't have wrecked my project. Ramón wouldn't have rescued it, and we might never have gotten together.*

She thought of all the pain she'd been through because of her choices in her relationship with Ramón. But at the same time, now she knew quality guys existed. You just had to wait for them. Yes, the time with Ramón had changed her—damaged her and taught her. And what did her friends think of Ramón for having sex with her? Did they think he was a preying pervert?

Jacie broke into her thoughts. "Earth to Solana. Where are you?"

"Just thinking." Solana paused. She took a deep breath. "Do you guys hate Ramón?"

"NO!" they chorused.

"I think he's the best guy you've ever gone out with," Jacie said.

"He showed you how you deserve to be treated," Becca told her. "I don't think you'll ever go back to dating the Camerons of this world."

Solana rolled her eyes. "I hope not."

"Me, too," Hannah said. "If you have to date, go out with good, intelligent guys who treat you well—with the exception of, well, you know . . ." Hannah blushed.

"I know," Solana said. "You don't have to say it." She turned around. "Tyler?" She looked squarely at him. "I want you to tell me the truth."

Tyler cleared his throat. "It's, well, even though I know you girls so well, it's hard to say something like this with all of you staring at me."

"Okay, we won't look," Jacie said, turning her head and covering her eyes with her hand. "Is that better?" Becca and Hannah both turned away and hid their eyes.

"I'm going to look," Solana said. "I asked him the question."

"It's that . . ." Tyler faltered again.

"Spit it out!" Solana said.

"God made guys a certain way," Tyler said. "And Ramón is a guy. So I don't fault him for wanting that with you. I think most guys who aren't Christians think that sex is a normal part of any boyfriend-girlfriend relationship. It doesn't make it right, but Ramón doesn't live by the same code that I do. So, considering that he's a worldly guy, who doesn't believe in what God says about waiting, yeah, I think he's a great guy. But don't get me wrong—I hope you don't get involved with him in that way again. I hope you don't give yourself away to *anyone* again, Sol. I just think you're too valuable to pass around."

Solana felt her heart melt. She threw her arms around Tyler's neck and squeezed. "You're the best."

"Oh, don't give him any ideas," Becca said.

"He'd have to do something for *all* of us to be the best," Jacie said, batting her eyelashes.

"Yeah," Hannah said, "like take us to Copperchino after school."

"Hannah, that's a great idea," Solana said. "Thanks, Tyler."

Tyler dropped his head into his hands. "How did I get myself into this?"

"That's one of the benefits of being the best," Jacie said.

Tyler shrugged. "Okay, then. After school. Two-thirty. My car."

"If we'd known it was going to be *that* easy," Hannah said, "we would have asked for the Copper Mining Company."

"Oh, brother." Tyler rolled his eyes. "Don't push it."

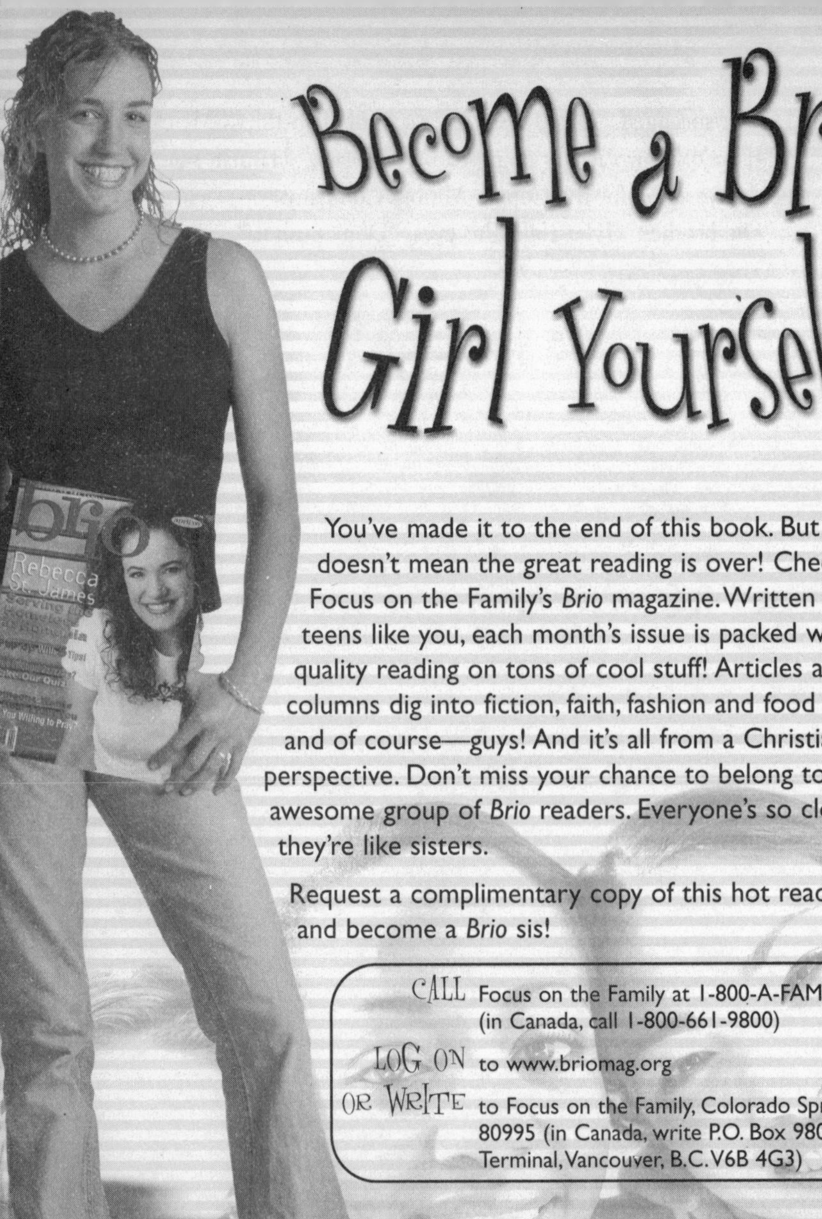
brio
Rebecca St. James
Become a Brio Girl Yourself!
You've made it to the end of this book. But that doesn't mean the great reading is over! Check out Focus on the Family's *Brio* magazine. Written for teens like you, each month's issue is packed with quality reading on tons of cool stuff! Articles and columns dig into fiction, faith, fashion and food . . . and of course—guys! And it's all from a Christian perspective. Don't miss your chance to belong to an awesome group of *Brio* readers. Everyone's so close, they're like sisters.
Request a complimentary copy of this hot read *today* and become a *Brio* sis!
CALL Focus on the Family at 1-800-A-FAMILY (in Canada, call 1-800-661-9800)
LOG ON to www.briomag.org
OR WRITE to Focus on the Family, Colorado Springs, CO 80995 (in Canada, write P.O. Box 9800, Stn. Terminal, Vancouver, B.C. V6B 4G3)
Mention that you saw this offer in the back of this book.